A Chorus of
Stuart M. K

"High opera and low comedy make a diverting mix in the fifteenth case for Toby Peters, Kaminsky's retro-detective . . . one of the best Peters outings."
> —*People*
>
> *

"Kaminsky has perfected his light touch . . . he proceeds effortlessly and in high good humor."
> —*Chicago Tribune*
>
> *

"The characters are amusing, the writing is camp, and the book is altogether entertaining."
> —*Kansas City Star*
>
> *

"The madcap plotting, celebrity appearances, and hard-boiled wisecracks produce more than their share of good moments."
> —*Booklist*
>
> *

"Mr. Kaminsky has such a good time writing, and he so loves the period, that the reader is swept along willy-nilly."
> —*New York Times Book Review*
>
> *

"Kaminsky's blending of fact with fiction is altogether delightful."
> —*Penthouse*
>
> *

"Stuart M. Kaminsky is a writer with the imagination of a Scheherazade."
> —*Washington Post Book World*

The Toby Peters Mysteries

· POOR ·
BUTTERFLY

A TOBY PETERS MYSTERY
STUART M. KAMINSKY

THE MYSTERIOUS PRESS
New York · Tokyo · Sweden · Milan
Published by Warner Books

Ⓦ A Time Warner Company

MYSTERIOUS PRESS EDITION

Cover design and illustration by Tom McKeveney

The Mysterious Press name and logo are trademarks of
Warner Books, Inc.

Mysterious Press books are published by
Warner Books, Inc.
666 Fifth Avenue
New York, New York 10103

A Time Warner Company

Printed in the United States of America

Originally published in hardcover by The Mysterious Press.
First Mysterious Press Paperback Printing: May, 1991

10 9 8 7 6 5 4 3 2 1

This is for Irene Bignardi, Giorgio Gosetti,
and Elisa Resegotti in Rome

with special thanks to
Sol Schoenbach, former First Bassoonist
with the Philadelphia Orchestra,
for his insights on Maestro Stokowski

Music is by nature remote from the tangible and visible things of life. I am hoping to intensify its mystery and eloquence and beauty.

—Leopold Stokowski

1

The chandelier couldn't hold our weight much longer. When Vera and I had climbed onto it, plaster had fallen and something inside the ceiling had breathed a sigh as if waking from a long bad dream. I'd pushed the ladder away as hard as I could, hoping it would fall without too much noise into the shadows and onto the pile of drop cloths, paint cans, and brushes the workmen had left there for the night.

The ladder had clattered, bounced a few times, and come to rest a few feet from the wall. I couldn't see it too clearly, but then neither would he if he came into the room. What little moonlight there was came from a trio of small round windows high on the wall.

Vera shifted her weight slightly, trying to feel secure—if not comfortable—twenty feet above the floor on a chandelier that shivered, groaned, and threatened to give way. We sat across from each other like two kids sharing a swing. Her legs were draped over mine and our hands clung to the pole that served to secure the mass of tinkling glass to the ceiling.

"Don't move," I whispered. If we didn't keep still, the tinkling would give us away if he came into the room. There was no electricity in this wing of the San Francisco Metropolitan Opera Building. It had been turned off for the renovation and repairs. He had a flashlight, but I was praying he wouldn't think of turning it upward unless we gave ourselves away.

He had a gun. It might take him four or five shots to dislodge us. If the shots didn't kill us, the fall would. And if the fall didn't, he'd be waiting for us with a choice of workmen's tools. I remembered how creative he had already proven himself on more than one victim in the past two days. I was beginning to think my choice of hiding places might not be a good one.

"It won't hold us, Toby," Vera whispered.

"It'll hold," I said with confidence, ignoring the creaking sound above and the fact that we suddenly dropped about an inch as the fixture's mooring sagged. More plaster falling. More tinkling of the glass doo-dads of the chandelier. Somewhere beyond the room an echoing of footsteps.

"Don't move," I repeated. "Don't talk. Try not to breathe."

The footsteps moved closer and I could hear him singing in Italian.

"It's from *Tosca*," Vera informed me. "He's singing Scarpia's aria of joy at torturing people in his secret room."

"Sounds like a fun opera," I whispered. "No more talking."

I wanted to reassure her, lean over and kiss her, hold her, but . . . the footsteps were drowned out by the singing; the voice was coming closer. I held my breath as the singing stopped. Silence. A long, cold silence and somewhere outside a distant car horn.

The first workmen would probably return to the room about eight or nine. I didn't know what time it was. Even if a beam of moonlight from one of the round windows hit my wrist, the watch I'd inherited from my old man would be no help. It never told the right time. It kept running, I'll give it that, but it had no interest in the time. Then I remembered the police had my watch. We were, in any case, a good three hours from the reasonable hope of any help.

The door below us burst open dramatically.

He sang something in Italian. Vera shuddered slightly, just slightly, as he stepped in. His voice, I hoped, covered the tinkling above him.

The flashlight beam touched the wall ahead. I didn't turn my head to look, just moved my eyes. The beam swept across wallpaper covered with little fat angels. Half the wall had been cleaned. Clean angels smirked at the still dirty ones. The beam moved left. His voice dropped. He was singing to himself now, with less of the confidence of the earlier aria.

I knew what he was thinking. He had to find us. The odds were in his favor. We were trapped in this wing of the old Opera building in San Francisco. The situation was simple. He had to kill us. If he didn't, we'd turn him in.

The beam kept moving. I had to turn my head slowly, slowly. The beam fell on the paint cans, brushes, and the ladder. The singing stopped as the beam went over the ladder, up and down, caressing it, considering it. And then he turned, his feet crunching fallen plaster, his beam searching the floor. I sensed he was directly below us.

He turned again, began to sing again, and moved to the door. The flashlight went out and the door closed.

Vera let out a very small sigh and took in dusty air. I did the same.

"I don't know if I can hold on till morning," she whispered.

"You won't have to." The voice came from below as a circle of light caught the thousands of pieces of glass and sent a rippling shadow over Vera's frightened face.

He laughed, a musical laugh, and I reached over to touch Vera's face as the laugh continued.

"Hold tight," I said to her.

My plan was simple, stupid, and almost certainly doomed to failure. I'd let go of the chandelier and jump toward the beam in the hope of landing on him. At this height I'd probably miss,

Even if I hit him, I'd be lucky to survive even if he didn't shoot me on the way down. I had just turned forty-six years old. My back was weak and I was tired. .

"Let's make a deal," I called down to him.

He laughed harder.

"You have nothing to deal with," he said. "Nothing. *Niente. Nada. No.*"

He started to move. Whatever chance I had would be gone if he moved out from under us to where I couldn't reach him.

"Tell me a story, a lie," he said, clearly enjoying himself. "Our Miss Tenatti can help you. Operas are filled with them. You left a secret note under the third stone step in front of the building identifying me as the Phantom. You confessed to a monk, a lawyer, a nun, who upon your death will denounce me. Thou art the man," he bellowed musically.

"What have you to trade for your lives? What will you give me? What?" he went on. "Your legacy? Title? Vera, you know the convention. Why don't you offer me your undying devotion in exchange for your lover's life? Then, later, you can kill yourself. I tell you both, this should be put to music. I hope you live long enough when you fall to say something. It would be too much to hope that Vera would be in good enough shape to sing one final aria as she lies dying in my arms. *Roméo et Juliette* would be fine. You know it, don't you, Vera?"

"Bastard," Vera shrieked in anger, setting the chandelier into frightened vibration.

"*Assassino*," he responded. "Call me everything. Sing to me one last time. We'll write a new end to the last act. Pinkerton finding Cio-cio-san dead of hari-kari took his own life in remorse, and *I* will sing the final aria over your bodies. Don't worry. I'll make it sad, poignant. A lament. Now what would be . . . *Lucia*. Yes. *Lucia*."

He shifted slightly. I'd have to jump soon. The circle of light hit the wall again. The cherubs were laughing at us. I didn't think he was close enough.

He was singing again.

"*Lucia*?" I asked.

"No," said Vera, "Canio's lament after he kills the lovers Nedda and Silvio."

Vera looked at me, saw me looking down, saw me let go with my left hand, sensed what I planned.

"I have one request," she said dramatically.

He stopped singing again.

"A last request," he said, intrigued.

"Come closer please," she said with a tear in her voice.

He moved closer, below us.

"Yes," he said. "You recall the last line of *I Pagliacci?* Canio says, 'The comedy is over.' "

"If I must die," said Vera, "let it be in silence rather than to the sound of a second-rate baritone who has neither resonance nor soul."

That did it. The flashlight beam probed through the glass, found us. The first shot shattered, sprayed. Bits of glass spewed, flew. Vera covered her eyes with one hand but she didn't scream. The bullet hit the chain of metal holding the chandelier, screamed, and thudded into the ceiling. My hand tingled from the vibration of the chain. Not much time. I took a fix on where he should be and let go.

My chest brushed the outside of the glass and played a tune as I fell. I could tell almost the instant I let go that there was no chance of my landing within two yards of the man who meant to kill us.

He bellowed with delight and the building shook.

2

It all started on a Friday in mid-December 1942. A woman who identified herself as Lorna Bartholomew called. Behind her a dog was yapping. The woman said, "Miguelito, be quiet," asked me if I was free to come to San Francisco immediately to take on an "assignment." The dog kept yapping.

It was raining in Los Angeles when she called. I'd been sitting in my office in the Farraday Building, looking out the window, feeling sorry for myself. Before the war I used to sail paper airplanes out the window on rainy days and watch them fight the elements on their way to the alleyway six floors below. But paper was scarce now. Kids collected it, tied it in bundles, and brought it to school in their wagons to contribute to the war effort. SAVE WASTE PAPER a khaki-uniformed soldier on a billboard told us as we drove down Wilshire. The soldier on the billboard had his arm around a little boy whose wagon was piled high with old copies of *Collier's* and the L.A. *Times*.

"Just one for old times," I told Dash the cat, who sat on my desk licking the waxed paper of the dime taco from Manny's we had just shared for early lunch. Dash was a big orange beast with a piece of his left ear missing and one eye that didn't want to work with the other one. He's been with me a few months now. I never thought of him as mine. I didn't want to own a cat. I didn't mind sharing my milk and Wheaties and cheap tacos with him, but I didn't want responsibility for his happiness. I'll give Dash credit. He didn't push me. I'd met Dash on a case. He more or less saved my life.

"Watch," I said, folding an ad I'd received the day before from a pair of optometrist brothers named Irick in Glendale who promised me better eyesight with their new lightweight glasses. I held up the work of aeronautic art for Dash's opinion.

Dash stopped licking his paw and watched me open the window, letting in the sounds of rain and traffic on Hoover. He knew something big was up. As I sailed the plane into the rain, Dash leaped to the windowsill. His head moved and at least one of his eyes was fixed on the plane, which swayed, looped, and glided down. Dash purred and watched.

"Pretty good, huh?" I said.

The plane landed somewhere beyond the junked Chevy. An alcoholic named Pettigrew usually slept in the Chevy, but he had gone south to Mexico for the winter.

Anyway, that plane going out the window was the highlight of my week till the phone call came.

Sheldon Minck, who rented me the one-window broom closet I called an office, had stuck his head in to announce the call. Sheldon was working on a little boy when the call came. Sheldon is a dentist. If I were really the civic-minded knight I want people to think I am, I would have spent my days in front of the outer door of our offices warning away the unwary, telling them to flee with their hands held tightly over their mouths to preserve whatever remained of the enamel they prized. But the rent was low, and I couldn't spend my life protecting an unwary public from the unsanitary creatures who lurked in thousands of offices throughout downtown Los

Angeles with certificates on their walls claiming they were qualified to pull teeth, collect money from insurance companies, make you a star, tell your fortune, take your picture, find you an orange grove in Lompoc you could turn into a gold mine, or locate your lost grandmother.

Shelly, his bald head gleaming with sweat, his chubby cheeks bouncing, his Dr. Pepper-bottle-bottom glasses slipping on his nose, opened the door and pointed his cigar at me with one hand and reached over to hand me the phone with his other. We'd gotten rid of one phone in the office. Cutting overhead.

"For you," he said. "Long distance. Frisco."

"Thanks," I said, taking the phone and waiting for him to back out of the room.

Shelly brushed an ash from his not very white smock and stood watching as I took the receiver.

"You have a patient, Shel," I said, putting my hand over the mouthpiece.

"A kid," said Sheldon, pursing his lips. "He can wait."

Dash was still standing on the windowsill, hoping for another plane.

"I'd like some privacy, Shel," I said.

"Privacy," he said with a smirk to the cat, who ignored him. "Big deals going on here. Do I tell you not to come into my office when I'm working on a patient?"

"No," I admitted.

"Okay," he said. Behind him the kid in the chair shifted. Shelly turned, afraid that this one would get away. "I thought we were partners."

"We're not partners, Sheldon. I rent a closet from you."

"Friends, then." He pushed his glasses back and looked over his shoulder at the kid.

"Something like that," I conceded.

Sheldon nodded, accepting the concession. "Can I tell you something? I don't like the cat."

"Sheldon, I've got a long-distance phone call," I reminded him.

"I know," he said. "I answered it. I don't like any cats. I like dogs less. Can't get their teeth clean no matter what . . ."

Something lit up within Sheldon Minck, D.D.S. "You know something. That gives me an idea."

"I'm pleased, Shel," I said. "Now can you . . . ?"

"I can't talk anymore, Toby. I've got a patient and an idea." He departed, closing the door behind him.

"Mr. Peters?" the woman's voice said. "Are you there?"

"Right," I said, looking up at the cracked ceiling. "I'm sorry. Things are busy here today."

Then she told me about the San Francisco job and asked if I could be there fast. Dash heard the dog barking and aimed a sincere hiss in the direction of the phone.

"I'll check my calendar," I said, and I did. I put the phone down and looked up at a three-year-old Sinclair Gas calendar my mechanic, No-Neck Arnie, had given me. It was turned to March 1939. Dash went for the downed phone and spat into it, at the dog. I pushed him away and picked up the phone again. "I can get away, but I'll have to do some calls and postpone a few cases. You'll have to cover all expenses and twenty-five dollars a day."

"I . . ." she began.

"Make that twenty dollars a day," I amended. "I'm giving pre-Christmas discounts, but I'll need a fifty-dollar retainer."

"That will be fine," she said. "Would you like to know what this is about?"

It's about twenty a day to a guy with fourteen bucks left, a guy who's seriously been considering a security job at Lockheed, I thought.

"Of course," I said.

"When can you get here?" she asked. "Pardon me. . . . Miguelito, be quiet." Miguelito ignored her.

"Sunday morning," I answered. "Where is 'here'?"

"Oh," she said, and put her hand over her mouthpiece. It

was my turn to wait. The rain was still coming down hard and gray. This time I looked up at the photograph of me, my brother Phil, my father, and our dog, Kaiser Wilhelm. I was ten in that picture. Phil was fifteen. My mother was dead. My father soon would be. No one knows what happened to Kaiser Wilhelm.

"The San Francisco Metropolitan Opera Building," she said. "Second floor. Main offices. Will ten o'clock be possible?"

"Inevitable," I said.

"It involves a rather delicate matter," she said softly. Someone interrupted her. There was a man's voice in the background. I couldn't make out the words. "Maestro Stokowski would like to provide the details himself when you arrive."

"Maestro Stokowski," I repeated. "Leopold Stokowski?"

"Yes."

"Ten, Sunday morning," I said. "I'll be there. I'd like the advance in cash when I get there. Now, give me a phone number I can check to be sure this isn't a bad joke. We get those in my business."

"Yes, of course." She gave me a number in San Francisco. I wrote it down. It's hard to write on waxed paper, but I've had experience.

I hung up first and looked at Dash.

"Want to go to San Francisco?" I asked.

He ignored me. I took it as enthusiastic agreement. I told him it might be better if he stayed home and slept.

I was back in business. I made a call to my ex-wife, Anne, to let her know I would be out of town for a while. She wasn't home. I called her at the travel agency in Beverly Hills where she'd recently gotten a job. Anne has been up and down with me, and then later with her second and now deceased husband, Ralph Howard. Howard had lived high and left her nothing much. At the age of forty Anne had pulled herself together, taken a couple of deep breaths, put on her makeup, and gone back to work. Her airline experience landed her the travel job. The woman who answered the phone said there was no Anne Peters working at the Intercontinental Travel Agency.

"How about Anne Howard?" I said.

"I think you may want Anne Mitzen," the woman suggested.

"Her maiden name was Mitzenmacher," I supplied.

"Really?" the woman said with no real interest.

"I used to be married to her," I explained.

"Fascinating," she said. "I'll get her."

Another pause. I heard the kid in Shelly's chair let out a small squeal. I tried to ignore it. Anne came on the line.

"Toby. How did you find me?"

"I'm a detective." I reminded her.

"Don't call me here again."

"You are voluptuous," I said.

"Toby." There was a warning in her voice.

Anne is a dark beauty, full bodied, with soft skin. She'd walked out on me a little over five years earlier when it was clear that I would never grow up and didn't want to. We had no kids and lots of regrets.

"I've got a job in San Francisco," I said. "Client's Leopold Stokowski."

Long pause while she decided whether to play along for a few more seconds, take me seriously, or just hang up.

"Leopold Stokowski," she repeated.

"You know, the conductor. The one on NBC. Did the dinosaur bit in *Fantasia?* We saw him in that movie *A Hundred Men and a Girl.*"

"I know who he is, Toby," she said. "You did not see that movie with me. We were divorced when that movie came out. It must have been someone else."

"There is no one else."

"Have a good trip," she said. "Try not to call me when you get back."

"I thought we were friends again," I said. Dash meowed and licked his lips, then he pushed his nose under my hand to get at the waxed paper.

"Let's put it this way," she said. "When I need your company, I'll call you."

"You're going with someone."

"Detective," she said.

"He's a detective?"

"No," she said with a sigh. "You're the detective. You figured it out. Congratulations. I've got to get back to work."

"Who is he?"

"Good-bye, Toby. Take care of yourself."

She hung up. I considered calling her back but patted Dash's head instead and got up. I came around the desk with the phone in hand and Dash at my feet. When I opened the door to Shelly's office, he was talking to the wide-eyed kid in the chair. The kid couldn't have been more than nine or ten. In Shelly's hand was a slightly rusted tool that looked like pliers with vampire teeth.

"Dogs," Shelly was saying to the kid. "You got a dog?"

The kid didn't have a dog. He had a cheek full of cotton and a frightened look in his eyes but no dog. He shook his head. No dog.

"Shel." I tried to interrupt, but he was pursuing a different voice inside his head.

"Know anyone who has a dog?" he asked the kid.

The kid thought furiously. His eyes darted back and forth. He wanted to give this man with pain in his hand the answer he wanted.

"My Aund Saurah," the kid mumbled. "She hah a gog. Barry."

"How's his breath?" asked Shelly, reaching over to open the boy's mouth for a close look.

"Breaff?" the kid said with Shelly's finger in his mouth.

"Smells like a sewer, right?" asked Shelly.

The kid shook his head in agreement.

"Thought so," said Shelly, standing straight and tapping the pliers in his palm. "How much you think your Aunt Slush would pay for a pill, something she could put in Harry's food to make his breath smell good."

"Aunt Saurah and Barry," the boy corrected cautiously through a mass of cotton.

"That's a non sequitur," said Shelly, pleased with himself. He looked at me for vocabulary credits. I smiled. I wanted something from Shelly.

"Barry bides," the kid said.

"So, he bites," responded Shelly, undeterred. "Is that any reason he should be allowed to smell like a cow's ass?"

"Sounds like a great idea to me, Shel," I said, trying to draw his attention. "I think you just got it from me."

He woke from his dream of a multimillion-dollar dog breath fortune. "I've been thinking about this for years," he insisted, pointing the pliers at me.

"Am I done?" asked the kid, pulling cotton from his mouth and throwing the bloody mess in the spit sink.

"Yeah, sure," said Shelly absently.

The kid threw off the dirty towel around his neck, jumped from the chair, and ran out the door.

"I'm going to San Francisco, Shel," I said. "Job for the Opera."

"Mildred *says* she likes opera." He looked past me at the door as if his wife, Mildred, would come bursting in, demanding that he clean up the mess. A few months earlier Mildred had run off with a Peter Lorre impersonator. I'd helped Shelly get her back and get her off a murder charge when the guy was killed. I thought Shelly was better off without her, but he still worshipped the ground she spat on.

"Maybe Mildred *really* likes opera," I said.

Shelly grunted. "I've got this chemical somewhere," he said, turning from me and walking to one of his grime-covered cabinets. "Salesman gave it to me. If it works on people, why not animals?"

"I need twenty bucks, Shel," I said.

He stopped in front of the cabinet, adjusted his glasses and cigar, and looked at me again.

"Five minutes ago we were barely acquainted. Now you want twenty bucks and we're friends."

"I didn't say we weren't friends. I said we weren't partners."

"I like to think of us like . . . Cagney and Pat O'Brien in *Crash Dive*," Shelly said.

"You're a visionary, Shel. I'll get an advance in San Francisco and send it back to you Monday."

Dash had jumped into the warm spot of the chair the little boy had vacated.

"No you won't. You'll forget. Someone will try to kill you or something and you'll forget." He pouted. "Money doesn't come that easily, Toby. Here's what that kid just paid me for pulling a tooth."

He dug into his pocket, came up with a crumpled piece of newspaper. He put his cigar in his mouth and placed the pliers on top of the cabinet where he'd be sure to forget he'd left them and opened the piece of newspaper to reveal two quarters.

"Shel, I *know* you've got money, remember."

"Twenty," he said, thinking about it. "In return for which you promise to give up all claim on my dog breath idea."

"You got it," I said.

He reached into his back pocket under his smock and came up with a wallet. He turned his back so I couldn't see, fished out a twenty, returned the wallet to his pocket, and turned to hold out a crumpled bill.

"Just a loan," he said.

"A loan," I agreed, taking the bill and putting it in my pocket. Shelly turned to his cabinet and opened it.

"I'll call," I said, moving to the door.

Shelly grunted.

Before I left the Farraday Building, I went to the office of Jeremy Butler, poet and former pro wrestler, who had for years fought the blight of bums and dirt that threatened to return the Farraday to the jungle.

Jeremy still put in his hours, but since his marriage to Alice Pallas, who almost matched him in size and strength, the Farraday had ceased to be his child. Alice was, in fact, pregnant, a phenomenon of some discussion in the Farraday since Jeremy was sixty-one years old and Alice, though she would not reveal her age, was certainly well over forty-five. I had attempted during one recent phone call to inspire Anne with Alice's example. Anne had hung up on me. Neither Alice nor Jeremy were in their office-apartment. It was still raining, but not hard, when I stepped out on Hoover and headed for No-Neck Arnie's garage on Ninth, where I parked my Crosley.

I made a deal with Arnie for a tankful and a ten-gallon can of gas for the trunk. It was black market, but this was an emergency. The gas would get me to San Francisco and back. Arnie opened the hood and gave the Crosley the okay for the trip. I gave him ten bucks. That left me twenty-four bucks.

The rain had stopped but the sky was still gray and grumbling when I left Dash in the car while I bought a wool sports jacket with zipper pockets at Hy's for Him, the Beverly Boulevard branch, for $4.99 plus tax. I picked up a pair of hot dogs from a stand shaped like a hot dog, ate one—dripping a minimum of mustard on the seat—and gave the other to Dash, who tore into it.

Ten minutes later I was parked in front of Mrs. Plaut's boarding house on Heliotrope. I went up the steps to greet my diminutive ancient landlady, who sat on a wicker chair, pencil in hand, writing on a lined pad. I had no doubt that the tome on which she labored was the massive history of the Plaut clan. It had become my responsibility to read and critique the manuscript; Mrs. Plaut was under the impression that I was alternately an exterminator and an editor. It was easier to live with Mrs. Plaut's delusions than to try to alter them. Mrs. Plaut had decided long before I met her not to accommodate herself to reality. All in all, she probably had the right idea. She looked up at me, down at Dash, and into the sky.

"Mr. Peelers," she said. "Rain and cats."

"Rain and cats," I agreed, taking a few steps across the porch. My goal was simple. Get to my room. Pack my few belongings, say good-bye to Gunther Wherthman if he was home—or leave him a note—and then head for San Francisco with Dash.

"Inspiring," she said with a deep sigh, tucking her pencil behind her ear, placing her pad of paper on the porch swing, and folding her hands on her flower-print dress. "I do not want your cat to eat my bird."

"He won't," I said.

"If your cat eats my bird, or attempts an assault upon my bird, I shall be forced to take the Mister's gun and demise him." She looked down at Dash with a smile.

"We understand," I said.

"No, Mr. Peelers," she corrected. "*You* understand and it is *your* responsibility. The cat understands very little. The cat is only a bit less dim than the bird."

"I'm going to San Francisco on business," I said. "I'll be gone for a while."

She tilted her head toward me and adjusted her hearing aid.

"To San Francisco," she repeated. "I was in San Francisco during the great earthquake. Mr. Spencer Tracy and Miss Jeanette MacDonald did not have the facts straight in their film. It was not Mrs. O'Leary's cow that started the earthquake. Mrs. O'Leary's cow started the fire in Chicago at an earlier time. But that is neither here nor there. Your Number Nine sugar stamp is good for three pounds till Tuesday. I assume you will have no use for it."

"I'll give it to you," I said, opening the door.

"I'll take it," she said. "And I will make Empire cookies or one of the cakes from Miss Marjorie Kinnan Rawlings' new *Cross Creek Cookery* book, which Mr. Hill gave me for my birthday. Some people remember birthdays."

"Mrs. Plaut," I said, letting Dash move in ahead of me. "Mister Wherthman and I gave you a new Arvin radio with headphones for your birthday." Mrs. Plaut's date of birth varied with her moods and memory. She had at least two birthdays each year, one in the spring and one at random times in the fall or winter. Her most recent birthday had been November 14, which, coincidentally, is my birthday.

"Be that as it may be. You will please take my recently finished chapter and place it in my hands upon your return with beneficial comments and criticism," she said. "That will be your part of the bargain."

I wasn't sure what her part of the bargain was, but I nodded in agreement. I hurried up the stairs and moved past the room of Mr. Hill the postman, past my own room, to the room of Gunther Wherthman.

Gunther is a little person, three feet of Swiss dignity. He is my best friend. I knocked. No answer. Gunther usually worked in his room, translating a variety of languages into English. Dash and I went into my room. It wasn't much but I liked it. I had a hot plate in the corner, a sink, a small refrigerator, some dishes, a table and three chairs, a rug, a bed with a purple blanket made by Mrs. Plaut that said GOD BLESS US EVERY ONE in pink stitching, and a sofa with little doilies on the arms that I was afraid to touch. On my wall was a Beech-Nut Gum wall clock that was never more than five minutes off.

I wrote a note to Gunther telling him I was going and asking him to take care of Dash and wind the clock. I knew Gunther wouldn't mind. Dash reminded him of a cat he'd had as a kid in Bern.

I packed what I had clean, which wasn't much. My one suit was slightly crumpled and not too dirty. I had a white shirt I'd only worn twice since the last washing, and three ties, all dark, one with a scorch mark on it that might be taken for a Scottish crest by a drunk.

I gave Dash some water. Gunther had told me not to give Dash milk. Milk, he said, was bad for cats. Gunther was usually right. I supposed it was some truth known only to Swiss midgets. I don't know what milk does to people, but I had enough left in the refrigerator for a bowl of cereal. I pulled out what was left of my Kellogg's Variety Package. It was a toss-up between Pep and Krumbles. I took the Krumbles.

I considered getting the mattress off the floor and back on the bed. I can't sleep in a real bed. Too soft. Bad back. I asked Dash's advice. He had none. I pulled the mattress up on the bed and checked the clock on the wall. It was getting late.

On my way out, I gave Mrs. Plaut my sugar stamps and she gave me her manuscript chapter, reminding me to guard it with my life.

"The chapter deals with my Cousin Pyle and his ilk," she said. "Therefore, it is especially precious."

She also warned me about loose women, cold weather, and something that sounded like "Crolly Beans."

The sun came through the clouds low on the horizon as I hit Sunset and headed for the highway and San Francisco.

3

Even under a bright morning sun, the San Francisco Metropolitan Opera Building looked like a tired old stone monster with sagging shoulders. It was in the wrong place, outside of downtown, within sight of the shipyards, tucked between a rotting warehouse that looked like a windowless airplane hangar and an empty lot with a peeling black-on-white sign yawning that this choice property was available for immediate development.

I parked behind a black limo in front of the building. A chauffeur about my size in gray uniform leaned against the car, his cap on the hood. He was reading a dime detective magazine, which now cost fifteen cents. A couple of men and a woman in overalls were patching holes in the dozen stone steps that led up to the main door of the building. They tried to pay no attention to the two old women and a man on the sidewalk carrying signs and walking patrol.

I read the signs as I moved toward the Opera. It was easy; all three turned their signs toward me. The closest, held up by an ancient rickety woman with a maniacal grin, read: NO WAGNER,

19

NO JAP OPERA. The second old woman's sign read: NO SYMPATHY, NO QUARTER FOR THE JAPANESE. The old man, in full suit and tie, a few wisps of unruly white hair dangling down his furrowed forehead, held up the final sign, which read: BUTTERFLY UNDERMINES AMERICAN RESOLVE. KILL JAPS, DON'T LOVE THEM.

"Sir," said the old man, "are you an American?"

"I'm a private detective," I replied, moving past them and up a few steps.

"That is an evasion," he shouted. "Reverend Souvaine says there is no room for evasion. Our nation is at war with a godless enemy."

"Amen," chorused the old lady picketers.

I went up the rest of the steps to the main door to the building. I stood for a few seconds trying to follow the twists and curls of the design covering the recently repainted wooden doors, then I went in.

I'd spent the night in one of the shacks they called motels out on the Pacific Coast Highway. Hundreds of these motels with cute names had sprung up on California highways and back roads since the war had started up. The second little pig had built a more sturdy home than the cabin of the California Palms Motor Hotel I had slept in the night before. Even with the windows closed and my radio playing Horace Heidt, I couldn't drown out the trio battling in Spanish in the next cabin. They fought till about three in the morning. Horace Heidt had long since put his baton away, and I had taken a shower in brownish, not very hot water.

So, I'd had little sleep. When I'd shaved a few hours ago, I was reasonably satisfied. My hair was reasonably short, with just enough gray in the sideburns to suggest I had been around long enough to know what I was doing. The battered nose and worn face indicated my knowledge of life hadn't come from books, and my new jacket with the zippered pockets suggested that, while I wasn't in on the latest styles, I could afford to keep out the Northern California cold.

I could tell as soon as I entered the dark entrance hall that the Opera building was bigger than it looked from the outside. I stood, letting my eyes adjust to the sudden change in light. Somewhere deep inside, far away, a woman's voice echoed in song. An orchestra brassed behind her.

"Like the sound of a finger run gently around the rim of a delicate English wineglass containing a perfect cabernet," a deep voice said in the darkness.

My eyes were adjusting, but I didn't look around for him. Instead I examined the walls, the ceiling that went up four stories. There were windows, high on the wall. They were papered over but light was coming through. I began to make out corners.

"Nice voice," I said.

"Hers or mine?" he said, stepping out of a deep shadow.

He was big, rather overweight, maybe my age. His dark hair was long, almost to his collar, and combed straight back. He was wearing a pair of dark pants and a dark sports jacket. A yellow polo shirt added color to his outfit. As he stepped closer, his hands clasped together as if he were about to launch into a solo, I could see his dark, smooth face. The little black beard and thin mustache made him look a little like a pudgy Mandrake the Magician. There was something familiar about the face.

"You recognize me perhaps?" he said.

"You've been in the movies," I said, putting my hands in the unzipped side pockets of my new jacket.

"A movie," he said, stepping still closer, "and . . . *shhh*." He held a ringed finger up to his lips to stop our conversation as the faraway voice of the woman rose, quivered. A smile crossed the man's face. His eyes closed. His head weaved. He was a ham. The aria ended. The woman's voice stopped.

"A movie," he resumed. "I'll sing again."

"You will?"

He chuckled. "*I'll Sing Again* was the name of the movie. I am Giancarlo Lunaire. Or at least I was Giancarlo Lunaire for twelve seasons, fourteen albums, and one very disastrous movie. Now I am, as I was born, John Lundeen."

He put out a hand and I shook it. I felt the metal of his rings cold against my fingers and saw the even line of large white teeth.

"You are, I am assuming, Toby Peters?"

"I am."

"Good, I wouldn't like to think I was wasting all this charm on a building contractor. Come. The Maestro is expecting you at . . ."

". . . ten," I supplied.

"Then we have a few minutes," he said, an arm around my shoulder, leading me down a corridor. He guided me to a wall and threw a switch. The place lit up. It looked like someone who had seen too many movies set in France before the Revolution had decorated it with vanilla frosting.

"Impressive, isn't it?" Lundeen said, sweeping his hand to invite me to take the whole thing in.

"Yeah," I said.

He led me down the corridor and pointed out curls and designs, little plaster figures nestled in niches papered with cherubs, and bare-breasted women carrying urns on their shoulders.

"This magnificent edifice was created by Samuel Varney Keel in the 1860s and seriously damaged in the 1906 earthquake. It was used as a storage warehouse until I convinced a group of patrons to reopen it. See those busts up there? The one with the broken nose?"

"I see it."

"Keel was obsessive. He created the busts with flaws. Every cherub, every figure, every design in this labyrinthine structure was carefully, lovingly designed to make it look European, but his sense of Europe knew no century. Unfortunately, Keel was eclectic."

"Eclectic," I repeated as we approached a set of wooden doors at the end of the corridor.

"Yes, he . . ." Lundeen began.

"Took his ideas from a lot of different places," I said.

"I apologize."

"What for?" I asked.

"Condescension," he said. "Can you forgive me?"

We had stopped. His hands were clasped in front of him. His head was tilted to one side. His smile was apologetic. A little of John Lundeen went a long way. I felt like blessing him before I gave him forgiveness.

"What's the job?"

"Ah, the job," Lundeen said, ushering me to one of the doors. "Millions have been invested in this structure. Millions. Including all of my own meager savings. Our investors wish less to realize a profit than to bring back the resplendence of grand opera in this noble edifice, to show the world that in these trying times, life, culture, and tradition can rise from the ashes and go on. We have the blessing of Mayor Rossi, Admiral King, many others, but we struggle, Mr. Peters. Ah, but we struggle. It is difficult to get skilled workmen during a war. Look around. You'll see women and old men with tools and paint brushes. This has proven to be a task far greater than we anticipated. And we must open in three days."

"The job," I repeated as he opened the door.

"Since you are the Maestro's idea, albeit a welcome one," he said, "I prefer that he explain."

I stepped into a theater that did more than hold its own with the rest of the building. The theater wasn't lit, but the stage to our left was. The light from the stage was enough to show a thousand or more seats and a balcony. There were even box seats set back above us. And one massive glass chandelier, catching what it could of the light, hung high above the seats.

On the stage were two people. One was a white-haired man about sixty in gray slacks and a long-sleeved gray pullover shirt. The sleeves were rolled up. He was talking to the second person, a woman who, for a second or two, looked like Anne. The body was similar—full, dark. The hair, too, was dark and full with—at this distance—a touch of red from the lights. She was wearing a blue dress with a big shiny black leather belt.

The man's fingers were dancing and the woman's head was nodding, her eyes fixed on him. An orchestra sat silently in the pit in front of the stage.

Lundeen moved ahead of me toward the front row. The white-haired man paid no attention to us. The woman glanced in our direction. The similarity to Anne was still there, but there were differences. This woman was probably still in her twenties. Her eyes were blue and her face smooth and childlike.

"Vulnerability," the white-haired man was saying. Actually, he said "vool-newr-ability." "If you fail to pro-ject vulnerability with determination and underlying strength," he told the woman, "you will give the character no depth. Your voice is an instrument like a fine violin. That you know. But you must coax more from it than perfect notes. This is opera. Performance. You comprehend?"

"Yes," she said, glancing at Lundeen and me as we sat. The seats were covered with some soft stuffed material.

Stokowski stepped back from the woman and looked at us for the first time. He was about six feet tall and stood erect, his eyes unblinking, finding my face. I smiled at him. He didn't smile back.

"I have a rehearsal this afternoon," he said over his shoulder to the young woman. "You work with Giancarlo and the tenor . . ."

"Martin Passacaglia," she muttered softly.

". . . if he arrives for rehearsal this afternoon," Stokowski concluded.

"Yes," she said dutifully.

"It's getting better," he said, his eyes still on me.

"Thank you," she said. She didn't seem sure whether she should stand there and wait for an escort or make her exit. A woman suddenly appeared from stage left, where she had probably been waiting, and beckoned to her. The woman was thin, dressed in a black suit, and of no clear age. She held a small white dog in her arms. I tagged her for Lorna Bartholomew and the mutt for Miguelito. I watched the two women exit.

Stokowski moved to the front of the stage, looked down at the orchestra for a moment, and pointed at a violinist.

"You," he said. "Do you have another instrument?"

"No," said the man.

"Leave," said Stokowski, walking to the end of the stage and coming down the stairs. "An inferior instrument cuts through my heart like the knife of a Prague butcher."

The violinist got up. He was about fifty and wore rimless glasses. He made his way out with as much dignity as he could muster while his fellow musicians looked at their own instruments, hoping they would not prove inferior, too.

"Overture," Stokowski said, stepping to the podium a few feet in front of where Lundeen and I were sitting. The Maestro raised his hands and began to conduct. He didn't use a baton. He didn't need one. His hands flowed. His fingers pointed. His lips moved.

There was no music in front of him. We sat silently and listened. It sounded great but I needed a coffee. I was afraid I'd fall asleep and he'd point his finger at me and tell me to take my inferior instrument home.

The overture ended. Stokowski sighed, shook his head, and said, "Oboe. You, oboe."

The oboe player, a very old man, looked up, ready to accept the ax.

"When I coax you with my hand like this," said Stokowski, demonstrating the hand movement, "I want you to play, to help. The flutes were lost. They have improved in quality in the last ten minutes but lost in volume."

"But," said the bewildered oboe player, his instrument cradled lovingly in his arms, "there was no music when you pointed at me to play."

"I am the conductor," said Stokowski. "If I point at you, coax you, it is because I need you, and you will play even if there is no part for you."

"You want me to improvise on Puccini?" asked the stunned old man, looking in the general direction of the string section.

"Yes," said Stokowski. "Yes. Yes if I need it."

"You want me to play . . . jazz?"

"I don't care what you call it," said Stokowski. "Just do it. Can you do it?"

"Yes," said the old man.

"Good," said Stokowski. "Practice."

"Practice what?" asked the old man.

"Creative flexibility."

With that Stokowski turned to us and looked at me. He was about three inches taller than me. He held out his hand and I took it. His grip was a lot firmer than Lundeen's. He waved for us to follow him as he left the podium and moved back toward the stage. The orchestra launched into a mess of sound.

"Opera is not my forte," Stokowski said loudly. "Nor is ballet or oratorio, though I have conducted them all. I have done them. My *Parsifal* was more than competent. It has been said that my *Wozzeck* was a triumph. What did Deems Taylor say of my *Wozzeck*?"

"He said it was a triumph of your career," Lundeen supplied cheerfully over the instruments as we reached the stage.

"Normally, I leave opera to Toscanini, and I hope that Toscanini will leave the symphony to me," Stokowski said, looking into the darkness at the rear of the theater as if expecting Toscanini himself to appear suddenly. "Are you familiar with my work, Mr. Peters?"

"I saw *100 Men and a Girl* once and *Fantasia* twice," I said. "Once with my nephews Nat and Dave. Nat liked the dinosaurs. The other time was with Carmen the cashier from Levy's Deli in Los Angeles. She liked the dancing hippos."

Stokowski smiled.

"Stravinsky lends himself to extravagance. Do you know

why you are here, Mr. Peters?" he asked. "Did Giancarlo tell you?"

"I thought you should do that, Maestro," Lundeen said nervously.

"Good," said Stokowski. "We'll talk on the way to my car. I'm expected at the presentation of the Congressional Medal of Honor this morning on the cruiser *San Francisco* to a young naval commander named McCandless, who is credited with taking over the task force during the Battle of Savo Island last month after his commander and his captain were killed and he himself injured. Commander McCandless, I understand, is thirty-one years old. Now if we add a waiting girl, we have the material for a modern patriotic opera. The car is waiting, Giancarlo?"

"I'll . . ." Lundeen stood up.

"Big black limo with teeth," I said. "It's waiting."

Stokowski strode to the end of the stage and went down the steps. We followed him and I wondered what the hell we had gone up onto the stage for.

"You come recommended by a mutual friend," Stokowski said as he walked up the aisle and out the door into the corridor. "Basil Rathbone. He and I recently did Prokofiev's *Peter and the Wolf* with the All-American Orchestra for Columbia Records. Basil said you could be trusted."

Stokowski walked briskly. I kept up. Lundeen had to work at it.

"The situation is this," he said. "Assuming this building can be made presentable, an opening performance of *Madame Butterfly* will take place in two days. I am skeptical. The young lady you saw me talking to, Vera . . ."

". . . Tenatti," Lundeen panted.

". . . will make her debut," said Stokowski. "Giancarlo and his board wanted Bidu Sayao, but she is doing another Puccini, *Manon*, at the Metropolitan in New York. This girl is passable. Promising. I will conduct on opening night only. I must get back to New York. I have a contract with NBC, but I have agreed to lend my support, advice, and name to this project. In exchange for this support, Giancarlo has graciously agreed not only to pay me a reasonable fee but to donate 50 percent of all profits during his first season to relief for refugee children in my name."

We were at the front door. Lundeen moved ahead of us to open it. Sunlight blinded us. I was looking at Stokowski. He didn't blink.

"Sounds great," I said. "And you want me to play Pinkerton?"

Stokowski laughed.

"You are already playing a Pinkerton and we have an operatic Pinkerton," he said. "A tenor named . . ."

". . . Passacaglia," Lundeen supplied.

"Tenors exist to be killed at the end of Act Two," sighed Stokowski. "In any case, he has done the role many times. He fancies himself more skilled than he is. You know opera?"

"Not really," I admitted as we stepped outside. "Knew a guy named Snick Farkas who worked in a gas station where I rode shotgun nights in Encino. Snick learned to love opera in prison. I also had a wife once who knew opera. *Butterfly* was her favorite."

"Unfortunately," said Stokowski, walking down the stone steps past the busy workmen, "there are some who find it an odious work. There are those who believe an opera which sympathetically depicts the plight of a Japanese woman abandoned by an American naval officer is unpatriotic. There are those who believe the opera should not be performed. There have been newspaper editorials . . . and these pickets."

We were approaching the limo now. The chauffeur had pocketed his novel and put his hat back on. He held the door open for Stokowski, who put his hand on the open door and turned to me. The temperature was about 60 degrees but Lundeen was sweating from the quick pace and the weight he was carrying.

The trio of ancient picketers was approaching us.

"Are you American?" the old man bellowed at Stokowski.

Stokowski sighed and met the old man's glaring eyes.

"I was born in Poland," he informed the man. "Spent my early years in England and have been a resident and citizen of the United States for a good many years. I am here by choice and not by an accident of birth. I am, as a good American, applying my talent and efforts to the winning of this war. I would think that you and these charming ladies would better serve the nation by collecting scrap paper or cans of fat, wrapping bandages, or selling Defense bonds and stamps instead of interfering with esthetic issues about which you clearly know nothing."

With that, Stokowski turned his back on the old man, whose eyes were darting back and forth in a delayed attempt to understand what had just been said to him.

"Show Mr. Peters the note, Giancarlo," Stokowski went on, looking over at my battered khaki Crosley.

The ignored picketers spotted a paint truck pulling up about twenty feet away and turned their attention to the two women in overalls and caps who were climbing out of the truck.

Lundeen stepped forward and reached into the pocket of his jacket. He had some trouble fishing out the envelope. It was slightly moist when he handed it to me. I opened it and pulled out a rough, thick sheet of paper. The note was handwritten in ink with fine curlicues. It was worthy of the guy named Keel, who had designed the monster we were standing in front of. I read it:

> Be advised. Be warned. Heed. This is a time of tempest and heat. Gods are watching. We are watching. Japan must not be glorified, its people idealized. We are at war. To present this opera is to be a traitor. In war, traitors are executed. All who participate in this abomination are traitors subject to execution.
>
> Erik

"Where did you find this?" I asked.

"Nailed to the door last Wednesday," said Lundeen, looking up at the door.

"You don't think it's a crackpot, a joke, a . . ." I said, but stopped when Lundeen shook his head.

"A man is dead, Mister Peters," Stokowski said.

"The day after the note was found," said Lundeen. "We were rehearsing. There was a scream. We hurried into the foyer and found a plasterer. He had fallen from the scaffolding."

"Fallen?"

Stokowski touched his high brow with his long fingers. They came away dry. "The man's name was Wyler. He was forty years old, sober, experienced. The scaffolding was secure. Giancarlo, Lorna, and another person saw someone wearing a cape climbing the scaffolding before Wyler fell. They paid no attention, thought it was someone going up to help with the plastering. We have checked with the plasterers. None of them climbed up to help Wyler that morning. The police are not interested. They believe it was an accident. They think I took advantage of a coincidence to build publicity."

"I can use the work," I said. "And I'll take it, but . . ."

"I received a call the morning after the unfortunate Mr. Wyler fell from the scaffolding," Stokowski said. "A raspy voice, a baritone possibly, said a single word, 'One,' and hung up. Perhaps it is coincidence, but since the police will not investigate, I thought it prudent to enlist your services both to protect the production and to identify this Erik. It is my hope that nothing is amiss. Is that your automobile?"

He was pointing at my Crosley.

"Yes," I said.

"I should like to ride in it at some point," he said. "Giancarlo will give you what you need."

With that he shook my hand, climbed into the back of the limo, and was gone.

"Well?" asked Lundeen.

"Twenty a day and expenses, like I told the lady on the

phone," I said, pocketing the note Lundeen had handed me. "And fifty for a retainer."

"That is most reasonable," he said. "Shall we go to my office and sign a contract?"

"Your word's good enough."

It wasn't that I trusted Lundeen, or even Stokowski. I've been stiffed by the poor and the unpoor alike, but a contract with the rich doesn't mean anything. You can't sue them. Even if you win, you'd be behind on lawyer fees. It's better to take your chances and give the impression that you trust people, even overweight people who sweat in cool weather.

"Thank you," said Lundeen.

"Two quick questions," I said. "First, you saw someone climbing up the scaffolding just before this Wyler fell?"

"A man in a black cape, which seemed odd, but this is a city of odd people," sighed Lundeen.

"Second question. Who's Erik?" I asked as we headed back up the steps.

Lundeen laughed, a deep laugh that made the workmen and women turn their heads in our direction.

"Erik," he said, "was the Phantom of the Opera."

4

Lundeen's office was on the second floor, up a flight of marble stairs. It had clean windows and furniture—old, heavy furniture. He handed me fifty dollars cash, plus sixty for my first three days. I was rich. He didn't want one but I wrote out a receipt. Now we were buddies.

Lundeen went behind his desk and sat down. I sat in front of the desk.

"Where do we begin?" he asked. "I've never done anything like this."

He began to fidget with the rings on his fingers. He stopped fidgeting and reached for a cigar in the humidor on his desk.

"I don't smoke in front of the Maestro," he said. "Would you like one?"

"No," I said.

He lit up and felt better. It wasn't an El Cheapo. I could take the smell for a while.

"We begin," I said, "with a list of everyone connected with this opera, everyone who might be a target."

"Then you believe . . ."

32

"No," I said. "But I'm being paid to act like I believe."

"The list is long," he said. "Contractors, musicians, office staff, cast, costume shop, set construction, lighting engineers. I'll get it for you."

"Put a check in front of the names of everyone who was here when Wyler fell," I said. "How many people were in the building that morning?"

Lundeen thought about it, looked at his cigar, belched out smoke.

"I don't know. A few dozen perhaps," he said. "No, more. The orchestra, but they were together in the auditorium when it happened. I remember . . ."

"Cross check," I told him. "Give me the names of everyone who was in the theater."

"I see. Whoever was with us rehearsing couldn't have killed Wyler."

"Unless more than one person is involved," I said. "The Erik note said, 'We are watching.'"

"The royal 'we,' perhaps," Lundeen said, pointing the cigar at me. "Or an allusion to his belief that he represents more than himself."

"Put a few people on it. Ask who was here. Ask them who they remember being here. See if someone remembers someone being here who claims he or she wasn't here."

"Elimination will lead us . . ." he began with enthusiasm.

". . . probably nowhere," I said. "But that's where we start. And we'll need people here twenty-four hours a day watching and protecting while I look for our playmate Erik. That'll cost."

"Since we stand to lose over two million dollars if we do not open *Butterfly* to reasonably good sales," he said, "we'll pay for protection. Do you have a service in mind?"

"I could bring my staff up from Los Angeles," I said, rubbing my chin, thinking about a bonus.

"Fine."

"We're a little unorthodox," I warned.

"So is an opera," Lundeen said, now rubbing his rings while he continued to puff at the El Perfecto.

"Let's say one week through opening night. Flat fee of five hundred dollars above what you're already paying me. If we have to go longer, we'll talk about it later."

"Sounds most reasonable."

"I'll get on it. Now I'd like a tour and an introduction to anyone around."

Lundeen walked me through the dark palace, through closed-off wings, into dark rooms filled with racks of costumes, props, and ancient light stands. Rows of dressing rooms, rehearsal rooms, offices, rooms filled with books, walls covered with paintings and posters demonstrated the master touch of old man Keel, who never knew when too much was too much. We passed some people working, painting, sweeping, but the dozen or so of them were lost in the vastness of the place.

"Impressive," I said.

"Expensive," Lundeen sighed. "It'll take years to fully restore it. The last opera performed here was *La Forza Del Destino* in 1904."

"Al Capone liked that one," I said as we walked.

"Al Capone?"

I didn't elaborate. I changed the subject.

"What was your specialty?" I asked as we moved into a hallway behind the stage that seemed to be in good shape and well lighted.

"Rossini, Massenet, Bizet, some Mozart, Puccini," he said. "I did a very credible Pinkerton in *Madame Butterfly* on a national tour in 1934, but I was considered too light, my voice too popular, for Wagner or even Verdi. I regretted the loss of Verdi, but not of Wagner. That I considered a blessing. Here."

We stopped in front of a dressing room door. There were voices behind it. Lundeen knocked. A woman said, "Come in."

In we went.

Vera Tenatti was seated in front of a mirror on a dressing

table, one of those mirrors with bulbs around it. Almost all the bulbs were working. A copy of *Woman's Day* lay on the table in front of her. Two cute white dogs looked up at her from the cover. The opera diva wasn't looking at the dogs. She was staring at herself, and she didn't look pleased by what she saw. An older woman in a dark suit, slender, blond—the woman who had led Vera off the stage—sat next to her, petting the little dog, who began yapping at me.

"Lorna Bartholomew, Vera Tenatti," Lundeen said, closing the door behind him. "This is Toby Peters, the investigator we've hired."

Lorna stood with a cool hand and a smile. She was polite, handsome, and somewhere else. The dog snapped at my hand.

"I talked to Mr. Peters on the phone," she said, releasing my hand. "I'm glad you could come. This is Miguelito. He's a miniature poodle with a very delicate temper."

"Charmed," I said.

"Vera?" Lorna touched the young woman's shoulder. The touch woke Vera from her fascination with her image and she turned.

"I'm fat," she said.

"I'm Peters," I said. "And you're not fat."

She looked at herself in the mirror again and repeated, "I'm fat."

"Occupational hazard," sighed Lundeen. "It takes a strong body, lungs to project. The body must be maintained like a fine instrument. There are no thin cellos. A thin cello would have no depth."

"It would be a violin," said Vera. "I would rather be a violin than a cello."

"I think you're cute," I said. "And you've got a great voice."

She turned from the mirror to look at me. I was telling the truth. She knew it. The smile was grateful.

"Mr. Peters simply wants to meet everyone," Lundeen

explained. "And to know if you remember where you were and who you saw last week when that workman died."

I pulled my pencil and small spiral notebook out of my pocket, ready to start putting things together.

"We were here," said Lorna, reaching for a black purse on the dressing table and fishing out a pack of Tareytons. "Stoki was here. A few plasterers, the orchestra, the principals. No chorus."

"The crazy old man," Vera added.

"Crazy old man?" I asked.

"Raymond," Lundeen said. "He came with the place. Caretaker. Knows where everything is. He was here before the place closed down in 1905. Makes little sense. He was with Lorna and me when Wyler fell. The three of us saw the man in the cape."

"I'd like to meet Raymond," I said.

Lundeen nodded. Since Lorna was standing and smoking, Lundeen took the opportunity to sit in the chair she and Miguelito had vacated. The wooden piece cringed under his weight but held.

"There were others," Lorna said. "But who remembers? We were rehearsing."

"Vera was in the middle of her second act solo," Lundeen added. "And Martin was . . ."

"Martin?" I asked.

"Passacaglia, the tenor," Lundeen explained. "He was in his dressing room, I think."

"He wasn't on stage," Lorna confirmed. "But neither was Pepe, the . . . who remembers?"

I put my notebook away.

"Do you need me for anything more?" Lorna said, looking into my eyes as she petted Miguelito. It was a Lana Turner line. She handled it so well I couldn't tell if she was being polite or encouraging.

"Not now," I said. "I'd like to talk to Miss Tenatti first."

Lorna shrugged a suit-yourself shrug. "John knows how

to reach me," she said, putting out her cigarette in a glass ashtray near Vera's elbow.

"I'll see you tomorrow, Vera."

She touched the girl's shoulder. Vera touched the older woman's hand and patted Miguelito's head. The dog liked it. Lorna departed.

"I do not like that dog," Lundeen muttered.

"He's a sweet dog," Vera said.

"I can pick it up on my own from here," I told Lundeen.

"Good. I'll be in my office most of the night," Lundeen said, moving to the door. "Do you think you can find your way back there?"

"I'm a detective," I reminded him.

He smiled and was gone.

"I've got some questions," I said to Vera, sitting in the now available chair and taking my notebook out again.

She shrugged and looked at me. Her eyes were wide, brown, and very deep.

"Yes." She gave me her attention.

"How old are you?"

"Twenty-nine."

"Twenty-nine," I said, writing in my notebook.

"Thirty-two," she amended.

I nodded, erased and wrote.

"How old are you?" she asked.

"Fifty."

"Fifty," she repeated.

"Forty-six," I said.

She laughed. It was a solid, beautiful, musical laugh.

"Where did you learn to sing?"

"St. Louis," she said. "I've been singing since I was four. You want to know my real name?"

"Sure."

"Vera Katz."

"Mine's Tobias Pevsner."

"Really?" she said, showing interest. I nodded and she went

on. "My mother was a singer. Local, light opera. My father was, is a music professor at Washington University. That's my life. Sing and get fat."

"You're not fat," I demurred. "You're very pretty and voluptuous."

She blushed.

"Brothers, sisters?"

"I was the only one. You?"

"A brother," I said. "Big, mean, a cop. You know what's going on here?"

"I've heard," she said with a shrug.

"You afraid?"

"No. Yes. A little. This is my big chance." She looked at herself in the mirror again. "Are there pudgy . . . voluptuous Japanese women?"

"Sure," I said.

"Maestro Stokowski says I should eat health food. I don't like health food. I like to cook. Look."

She opened the *Woman's Day* to a page with a folded corner.

"There are these great recipes for inexpensive cuts of meat," she said with enthusiasm, holding up a spread with six black-and-white pictures of plates of food. "Breaded fried tripe. Liver loaves. Brains in croustades. Heart patties."

"Let's get a cup of coffee and a carrot sandwich someplace," I suggested.

She looked at me differently now. "My father's fifty-two," she said.

"How old's your husband?"

"Don't have one."

"Boyfriend?" I asked.

She shook her head no, but the no was not emphatic.

"Martin has taken me out to dinner twice," she said.

"The tenor."

"Yes," she said. "But I don't think it's . . . and he has a wife in New York."

"How about that carrot sandwich?"

She nodded and smiled, a smile like the full moon.

It was a great moment. It would have been nice to hold onto it for a few seconds longer, but the scream ended it—a scream that seemed to cut through a dream, like the sound that wakes you from a deep sleep, a sound you're not quite sure is in the room or in your imagination. I looked at Vera. Her eyes had gone wide. She'd heard it, too.

I got up and went out the door. Vera came after me.

I needed another scream to know which way to turn. It came. From my right. I went after it. Vera was doing a good job of keeping up with me. There wasn't much light, and workmen had set up shadowed booby traps—piles of brick, boards, planks, tools—for us to trip over. Another scream guided us.

We hit the mezzanine corridor, which had no light but did catch some of the sun from the lobby. No more screams, but someone was running, shoes clapping on marble, heading up stairs, sobbing. When I reached the stairway with Vera a few steps behind, Lorna Bartholomew plowed into me, clutching her throat. I staggered backward. Vera caught us. We all went down. A white ball of fur scuttled across the floor and landed on my face.

"He . . . he . . ." Lorna gulped, looking back over her shoulder in the direction of the lobby.

I got to my knees, pushed Miguelito off my face, and helped her up. The shoulder pads in her suit had shifted. She looked like Joan Crawford doing Quasimodo. I reached over to help Vera, but she was up before us. Lundeen and another man came thundering along the mezzanine lobby behind us.

"He . . . he . . ." Lorna tried again.

"What's she laughing at?" the man with Lundeen asked.

"She's not laughing," said Vera. "She's frightened."

Vera moved past me to put an arm around Lorna's misplaced shoulders. Miguelito was yapping at her feet. Vera reached down, picked up the dog, and handed him to Lorna, who buried her face in his white fur.

"Are you all right?" Lundeen asked. He was panting. He looked worse than Lorna.

". . . tried to . . . He grabbed, put something around my neck," Lorna said, touching her neck with her fingers. Her neck looked bruised, marked with purple, yellow, and red. "I think Miguelito bit him."

"Something's there, all right," volunteered the old man with Lundeen.

"Where?" cried Lorna, looking around in fear.

"Round your neck," said the man. "Red mark. Snakelike."

I looked at the helpful old man. He was thin, with a mane of white hair over a surprised, chinless Slim Summerville pale face. Under his faded overalls he wore a reasonably clean white shirt and a yellow tie. He moved in close to examine Lorna's neck.

"Nasty, nasty," he said, shaking his head. "Saw things like that in the war against Villa. Mexes'd come up on us at night from behind like and take this wire around a neck and . . ."

"Raymond," Lundeen warned, trying to catch his breath.

". . . like a salami," Raymond trailed off.

"Get her some water," Lundeen ordered. "Get me some water."

Lorna was hyperventilating now.

"Make sense," Raymond snorted, shaking his head. "Water's not turned on up here. Got to go downstairs, find some glasses, clean 'em out, fill 'em up, juggle 'em up here. I'll lose most of it. You could get over to the Longshore Bar before I'd be back."

Lorna groaned and rubbed her cheek against the little dog. Vera helped her toward a marble bench against the wall.

"Get the water, Raymond," Lundeen insisted, moving to help Vera with Lorna.

"I'll miss something," Raymond complained.

"I'll bring you up to date," I promised.

Raymond shuffled off, hands plunged deeply into his overall pockets.

Lorna was sitting on the bench leaning against Vera when I reached the three of them. There was enough room for Lundeen, but he was standing.

"He came up behind me," Lorna gasped. "I was . . . from under the staircase. From the right. No, the left. I didn't hear . . . well, maybe I heard . . . something. Then it, something was around my neck. My purse. I dropped my purse."

She looked around for her purse. Vera showed her it was still on the strap around her neck.

"I screamed," she said. "I could smell his breath. Sickening. Sweet. My head bumped against his face." She shuddered. "His face was . . . hard. I think Miguelito bit him. Then he was gone."

"I'll call the police," Lundeen said, turning.

"The police," Lorna cried. "What will they do? They'll say I did it myself, that we're looking for publicity. If they wouldn't believe Leopold Stokowski, they certainly won't believe me. The only thing that would make them believe is my dead body."

Anger was taking over, masking the fear. I'd seen it before. It was safer to be angry than frightened. She would turn into attacker instead of victim.

"You," she said, looking at me. "You're supposed to protect us."

"Lorna." Vera said, "Mr. Peters has only been on the job a few minutes."

"I'm telling the Maestro," Lorna said, pulling at her purse, snapping it open with shaking fingers and finding her cigarettes. She pulled one out without noticing that it was bent and accepted the light from Lundeen's instantly produced lighter.

"Good idea," I said. "Miss Bartholomew is right about the police. They'll ask questions and go home. You need a clear felony to capture their interest."

"Shouldn't we lock the doors. Search the . . ." Vera began. Lunden was doing better with his wind now. "Too many exits. Too many places to hide," he said, shaking his head. "Too many people with a reason to be here."

At first I thought the sound was a workman humming. I wasn't sure when it started. It got louder, closer. Lundeen kept talking, gesturing, expounding on the futility of any defined course of action.

Vera heard it now. A voice, a man's voice, singing.

Lorna looked up. "What's that?"

"What?" asked Lundeen.

"The voice," Vera said.

Lundeen listened now. The voice was loud.

"It's him," Lorna cried, standing again, looking around. Vera comforted her. Miguelito growled.

"It's just a workman, a . . ." Lundeen started, but the voice grew louder.

"What's he singing?" I asked, trying to figure out where the sound was coming from. I moved toward a men's room door down the hall.

"It's from Verdi's *Un Ballo in Maschera*. Renato's lament after mistakenly killing his friend Richard," Lundeen said.

"Where is it coming from?" I shouted, and the music stopped instantly, mid-note.

I sensed someone behind me in the shadow. I went down low and started to come up with a right. Raymond jumped back, dropping a glass and sending a splash of water over my pants.

"I'm not going for more," he said, stepping into the dim light.

I opened the bathroom door. A small, temporary light bulb dangled from the ceiling. All the stalls but one were open. I wasn't carrying my gun. I usually didn't. It nestled in my glove compartment, where it couldn't hurt anyone. I'm not a particularly good shot anyway; I've been shot by that gun more than anyone else. I moved slowly, back to the wall. Outside the door I could hear Lundeen giving Raymond a hard time. Inside the bathroom I was giving myself a sweat.

Something moved behind the closed stall, something alive. The stall door went down to the floor. Hell, it was probably just a plastered plasterer taking a . . . I looked for something to bash him with, but there wasn't much in the way of choice. I picked up a piece of broken wood with a semi-serious jagged end. If I unleashed a vampire, maybe I could draw some blood. I took a breath, stepped in front of the door, and kicked it open. Something moved inside, a flicker. The door banged closed and slowly started to creak open again. A large, dark butterfly fluttered past me and drifted past the single open bulb.

I pulled myself together and went back out into the hallway. Vera was handing a glass of water to Lorna. Raymond was looking at me, one hand plunged deep in his pocket, the other holding an empty and not particularly clean-looking glass. Lundeen was seated next to Lorna.

"Nothing in there," I said, "but a butterfly."

"This is ridiculous," Lundeen said, turning around. "Someone is trying to frighten us.

"Doing a good job, too, from the looks of all of you," Raymond retorted. "Got you shadow-scared. I've been alone in this building every day for the past thirty-four years and never saw nor heard anything except Milo, the Furs, and the Ghost till you people came."

"Milo and the Furs?" Lundeen asked.

"Ghost?" asked Vera.

"Snakes, rats," Raymond explained. "Ghost been here since the place closed. Doesn't bother anyone."

"Who paid you all those years?" I asked.

"Providence," said Raymond, winking at me and holding up the empty glass in a toast.

"Providence hell," bellowed Lundeen. "I thought the real estate company paid you. But when I have the final inventory I'm sure it will confirm . . . You've sold off all the paintings, every piece of sculpture, every vase, every chair, every . . ."

"Plenty left," Raymond said. "It was all ugly as a horse's heinie anyway."

"You are fired," Lundeen cried.

"Ha," said Raymond. "I repeat, ha. I could damn well say it all night and into next Tuesday. I don't work for you. Kick me out and you won't be able to find anything in this place. I've got the keys and the know-how."

"Lundeen," I said. "Raymond's not the problem."

"I'm getting out of here," said Lorna, standing up.

"I'll take you home, Lorna," Vera said, giving me an apologetic smile.

I turned to the old caretaker. "Raymond, will you please escort the ladies to the front door."

"Certainly." Raymond handed Lundeen the empty glass and took Lorna's arm. Miguelito let out a single yap in Raymond's direction and then settled back in Lorna Bartholomew's arms. "All you gotta do is ask polite."

Lundeen sat deflated. I moved to the railing and watched Vera and Raymond help Lorna down.

"Erik," Lundeen sighed. "I tell you, Peters, the world is populated by lunatics. This war breeds fanatics. You'd think people would have enough to worry about without fixing their delusions on an opera. Why isn't he . . ."

". . . or they," I corrected.

"Or they," he agreed, "in the army or navy, fighting the Japanese, if they are so . . . I'm sorry. How would you know?"

"Maybe I'll find out," I said. "Round up everyone you can find in the building and bring them back into the theater. Ask them where they've been for the past fifteen minutes. Ask them for the names of anyone who was with them or saw them during the last fifteen minutes."

"You mean workmen? Contracting people? Pull them off work? Stop construction? Are you crazy?"

"Yes. Yes. Yes. Yes. And I don't know," I answered.

Lundeen shook his head and smiled, the smile of a martyr.

"All right," he said, getting up.

I watched him sway down the stairway, then I headed back into the men's room. I took two minutes to search it. No doors, no panels, nothing. Back in the hall I thought I heard a sound. I headed across the hallway to one of the doors marked MEZZANINE. I opened it and stepped into darkness and the smell of mildewed carpet.

The theater was quiet. The door closed behind me. I stood, trying not to move, listening.

"Poor butterfly." The man's voice came from above, echoing.

I listened quietly and when he finished the song with, "you just must die, poor butterfly," I applauded slowly, without enthusiasm.

"You jest," came the voice.

"When I can," I called out. "Did you kill the plasterer?"

"His name was Wyler," the voice said. "To you he was just a plasterer, but he and I were very close for a brief period."

"You killed him," I said, trying to get a fix on the voice.

"I gave him the opportunity to see if he could fly," said the voice. "He was unable to do so. Close the doors or the butterfly dies. It would be a shame for our beautiful diva butterfly to have such a short life."

"Buddy," I said, "you are a ham."

"On wry," he called back and laughed.

I wasn't sure I got the joke. I wouldn't have laughed even if I had.

"I'm on a daily retainer," I said. "Give me a run for my money so I can make it worthwhile. Don't make it too easy to find you."

"We won't," he said. "You'll see me soon. Ah, wait. A present before I take my leave."

Something whirled from the darkness under the boxes across from where I was standing. Whatever it was flew toward me. I moved to my right and the thing hit the wall of the box and clattered to the floor. I got up and looked over the railing.

I thought I saw a figure, black against black. I know I heard a door close.

I considered getting out, down the stairs and after him, but I knew I had no chance. Instead I reached down and picked up the ax Erik had thrown. The light was bad, but even in the dimness I could see there was something wet and sticky on the blade. I had a few guesses about what it might be.

5

It was late afternoon when Lundeen and I and a young woman named Gwen, who seemed to have no lips and eyes twice the size of normal behind thick glasses, put together the notes on where everyone in the building said they were when Lorna Bartholomew was attacked. Gwen, in addition to having no lips, had no breasts and no sense of humor. She was, Lundeen explained, a volunteer, a graduate student of music history at the University of San Francisco. Gwen was wearing a green dress with puffy shoulders and ruffles around the collar.

We were sitting in Lundeen's office at his conference table. Lundeen needed a shave and a new tie or a thinner neck. He kept shaking his head at the pile of papers. I had already called Los Angeles and told my "team of agents" to get to San Francisco by the next morning.

"Gwen," I said.

She looked up from putting the scraps of paper into neat piles.

"Yes," she said, giving me her full attention.

47

"You know what to do?"

"Yes," she said. "I'm checking alibis. And you want me to see who, if anyone, doesn't have reasonable corroboration, an alibi, for the period in question. You'd like me to do the same for the period in which Mr. Wyler the plasterer died. In that case, I am to determine who was at the rehearsal."

Lundeen looked at the girl hopefully. Perhaps she would solve all of his problems. The police had certainly failed to solve any of them.

After Erik had heaved the ax, Lundeen had insisted on calling the authorities. About twenty minutes later a pair of cops were ushered by Raymond into the mezzanine box where Lundeen and I were waiting. On the main floor, about forty people were gathered, waiting to find out why they had been called. The workers weren't complaining. They were paid by the hour. Some of the opera staff were grumbling. There were no musicians around. Lundeen assured me there was no way he could have kept any musicians sitting around waiting for the police.

The two cops asked who we were, where they could get more light, and why the auditorium was full of people. Raymond shuffled off to turn on the lights.

"Old guy's nuts," said one of the cops, who identified himself—when urged by me—as Sergeant Preston. Sergeant Preston had a craggy face and a thin body with a little cop gut. He wore a suit and the suit was clean, but it should have been turned in to the Salvation Army for rags.

"Nuts," agreed his partner, a big man with a constant smile and rapidly thinning blond hair who introduced himself as Inspector Sunset. Sunset's suit had a few years left in it.

They listened to our story. Sunset took a few notes, enough to keep us from claiming he wasn't paying attention. Preston listened but with no real interest. He was looking over the railing at the people below. After he'd listened to our story, Sunset looked down at the ax.

"Never been to an opera," Preston said.

"I have," said Sunset. "On the carrier *Forrestall*. Don't remember what it was. We thought it was going to be scary, about bats. Fat guy sang in German."

"That fat guy was me," Lundeen said. He had been sitting on one of the plush but dusty chairs. Now he stood.

Sunset looked over at him as the full lights went on.

"Fact?" he said

"You can put it in your notebook," Lundeen assured him. "And I weighed no more than two-twenty when I gave that performance."

"None of my business," said Sunset with a smile, looking down at the ax and seeing it now in better light. "Looks like blood all right."

"Take it in for Grunding," said Preston, still looking over the railing. "And get their statements. Standing here looking down makes you want to give a speech. You know, I did a little singing when I was just starting on the force?"

"Yeah?" said Sunset with genuine interest.

"Crooning," said Preston, turning from the railing, looking at Lundeen. "No opera."

"No opera?" Lundeen said. "Pity. Then we have less in common than I had hoped."

"Just for the police shows, kids—even got on the radio once."

"You think we might talk about murder, attempted murder?" I interjected.

Preston gave me a sour look and glanced at Sunset, who shrugged as he picked up the ax with a handkerchief.

"A man named Wyler was killed here a few days ago," I said. "And today someone tried to kill me with that and strangle Leopold Stokowski's assistant, Lorna Bartholomew."

"So you said," sighed Preston. "Voices, butterflies, phantoms. I saw the movie. Claude Rains, Nelson Eddy. Now that's a great singer."

Lundeen groaned. "Nelson Eddy is a flat baritone," he said.

"Sounds fine to me and the wife," said Preston.

"You and your wife . . ." Lundeen started, but I interrupted him.

"You have witnesses, Sergeant," I said, knowing where we would get before we got there.

"Witnesses," said Preston, moving back to the railing. "The plasterer fell. No one was there. The Bartholomew woman might be having her period or something and you, you're getting paid to hear voices and find murder weapons. Five will get you ten that's not human blood on that ax."

"It's not," Sunset agreed.

"Show business people have imaginations," said Preston. "I'll give you that."

That was about the time Raymond returned and asked, "I miss anything?"

"The 1930s," I said.

Preston chuckled. "You got a sense of humor," he said. "I like that. Let's go, Al."

"Let's . . . that's it?" asked Lundeen, looking at me. "What about protection? Investiga . . . Why don't you go down and question everyone?"

"Not the way it works," said Preston, nodding to Sunset to head for the door. "Put a little evidence together here. A body or two with a bullet or knife wound and we'll talk business. You," he continued, pointing at me. "Come with us for a second."

I followed the two cops out into the hall. Raymond started to follow but was waved back in by Sunset, who closed the door with one hand and held the ax with the other. He didn't seem to be worrying about blood or fingerprints anymore. He lifted the ax up like a bat and began to swing at pitches from a Yankee down the hall. Preston came close enough so that I could smell his Sen-Sen.

"Peters," he said. "Cut the shit. Tell these people to get their publicity some other way besides finding phantoms."

"No shit here, Preston," I said.

"We wouldn't even be here if the Captain wasn't afraid

Stokowski would raise a stink," he said. "And I don't want to come back. We understand each other?"

"You want a murder," I said.

"It helps," he agreed. "Aren't you a little old for this kind of garbage?"

"Aren't you a little old to still be a sergeant?" I asked.

"Yeah," he agreed. "Wife thinks it's the name. You know, Sergeant Preston of the Yukon. Thinks the Captain won't put me in for a promotion because he likes making the joke. I don't contradict the wife, but the truth is I'm a mediocre cop waiting to collect pension. That's just between you and me, right? I don't want trouble."

"Picked a strange profession," I said.

"Poor vocational counseling," he agreed. "Sunset should have been a ballplayer."

We looked at the smiling Sunset wacking an imaginary homer into the right-field stands.

"But he took shrapnel in his shoulder back in the Battle of Midway," Preston whispered. "He'll just have to settle for being a cop."

"Look," Sunset said. "Mel Ott." He set his feet wide apart and held the ax up high.

"You see where Branch Rickey just announced that the Dodgers were paying the Phils thirty thousand for Rube Melton? I could hit Melton. I could hit any right-hander last year."

"I know," Preston said. "Let's get back to work. Crime is running rampant in the streets."

That had been three hours earlier. They left, Lundeen sighed, then found Gwen and went down to interview the company and workmen.

It was a little after four when I left Lundeen, assuring him that the opera company was in good hands.

On the way down from Lundeen's office I listened for footsteps, butterflies, and music, but heard none.

Raymond caught me in the lower lobby.

"Big nose and beard, little pointy red beard," he said, stroking an imaginary beard under his chin.

"The Phantom?" I asked, walking on.

"Damned right," he said.

I thought you didn't get out much?" I said.

"Not much," he said, gangling after me as I hit the doors to the outside.

"That's the description of the Phantom the opera director gives in the movie," I said.

"Coincidence," said Raymond.

"Why you wearing a shirt and tie and overalls, Raymond?" I tried.

He looked down at himself as if this were startling news.

"Want to look my best," he said. "Make a good impression. Big things going on. Good-looking women. Want to keep working here when they pack up and leave."

"You don't think the opera is staying?" I asked, opening the door and looking down. One of the old lady pickets was gone, but the old man and the other woman were still holding their placards high.

"Nope," Raymond said. "Smell funny in here to you?"

I sniffed.

"Plastery-like," Raymond went on with a shiver. "Building liked itself the way it was. It was sleeping peaceful. Now they're waking it up. It'll get all this dust in its ducts and sneeze everyone out of here."

"Except you," I said.

"Probably," he agreed. "I know places to get a good hold when the sneezing starts."

"You're a poet, Raymond."

"Creativity runs in the family," he said. "Father was a trumpet player. Got me my job here back when I came back from fighting Villa. Goin' to rain."

"Looks like," I said. Raymond ducked back into the building, and I went down the steps right toward the old man with the placard.

"Got a question," I said to him when I reached the sidewalk.

He was wary, but any attention was better than what he was getting from the departing workers. The old woman looked at me hopefully and put down her sign.

"Got an answer," the old man said. "And the answer is quit this place and help convince others to do the same."

"Wrong answer," I said. "You mentioned a Reverend . . . ?"

". . . Souvaine," the old woman piped in.

The old man gave her a look of distinct rebuke.

"I am the on-site spokesman, Cynthia," he said to her.

Cynthia looked properly put in her place.

"I'm sorry, Sloane," she said.

"The Reverend Souvaine is the spearhead of God in the battle against the godless," said the old man, looking up to God with a small, knowing smile. God spat a few drops in his face.

"Getting God and politics a little mixed up, aren't you?" I asked.

"They are, as the Reverend Souvaine points out, inseparable," said the old man, looking at the woman, who nodded her approval.

"How do I find the Reverend?" I asked.

"He does not hide," said the man.

"Amen," said the woman.

A pair of women leaving the Opera looked over at us, then pretended to return to an absorbing conversation.

"Where doesn't he hide? Where do I find him?"

"Church of the Enlightened Patriots," replied Sloane. He reached into his back pocket and came out with a crumpled sheet of paper announcing an open meeting at the church. The date had passed, but the address and telephone number were there.

"Think it would be a good idea to get the lady off the street and get her a glass of iced tea?" I suggested. "It's starting to rain."

The man cocked his head to one side and looked at me with new eyes. The madness passed.

"The work of the church is Cynthia's and my life," he said softly. "It gives us meaning, purpose. Cynthia has not been well and doesn't have . . . We will stay till there is no one left in the building whose mind and soul we might still touch by the truth."

"Sure?" I asked. "I could give you a ride to the church."

"I'm sure," he said, and the madness was back. "We are sure. Have we touched your soul? Is that why you wish to see the Reverend?" There was hope in his question.

"You've aroused my interest," I said. "I'd like the Reverend to give me some more information."

"Amen," said Cynthia.

"Amen," I added.

The old man gave me directions to the Church of the Enlightened Patriots and I headed for my Crosley.

I'd left the windows open a crack. The crack had been enough for the Reverend's trio to stuff through a handful of leaflets. I put them in a pile on the seat next to me, started the Crosley, and went out in search of the church.

I found the Church of the Enlightened Patriots on an intersection just outside Chinatown. I was impressed. It was a red brick building with two sides curving down from a central clock tower. Above the clock was a carillon. At the top of the central tower were four crosses, one facing each direction, and a pinnacle with a bigger cross. I got out of the Crosley, waited for a streetcar to pass, and started up the stone steps before I saw that I had the wrong building. Above the door was written: OLD SAINT MARY'S CHURCH. I stopped a Chinese woman who was hurrying down the steps clutching a black patent leather purse to her breasts and asked her for the Church of the Enlightened Patriots. She pointed to the next corner and made a sharp gesture to the right to indicate a turn. Before I could thank her, she was gone.

I went down the street she had pointed to and found the

church. It looked as if it had gone through a few changes. It was a wooden two-story building painted white, with a wooden sign with black lettering announcing that this was the church and the Reverend Adam Souvaine was the pastor. There was no parking lot next to the church, which was wedged in next to a second-hand bookstore and a four-story office building whose sign, twice as big as that of the church, announced that there were vacancies.

It was after five and the street was empty except for a few cars parked along the curb. It was raining lightly. I locked the Crosley and found a burger joint half a block away.

The joint was small and clean with white tile floors and swivel stools at the counter, where you could see the grill. A few customers were chomping burgers and downing coffee or cola. I sat at the counter, where someone had left a copy of the San Francisco *Chronicle*. I ordered a Pepsi and a burger from the old Chinese guy in the white cap and apron sweating at the grill and learned that the Allies were repelling new tank attacks in Tunisia and that our planes were hitting Naples, Turin, and Rouen. The British had opened a new drive in Libya, and the Nazis were admitting that their defenses had been pierced.

"Nazis been pushed back more than seven hundred miles from El Alamein," the sweating guy behind the counter said, handing me the Pepsi.

"Montgomery's a tough fart," said a burly guy in a plaid shirt at the end of the counter. "Even if he does talk snooty."

"British all talk that way," the grill guy said, turning to my sizzling burger.

"No they don't," the plaid shirt said. "I work with a guy from London or someplace, and he don't talk like that."

"Like it rare or what?" the grill guy asked me.

"Or what," I answered.

He nodded.

"Know the church down the street?" I asked. "Church of the Enlightened Patriots?"

The plaid guy laughed.

"What about it?" The grill guy stopped to wipe his hands on his apron.

"The guy who runs it," I said. "He ever come in here?"

"Nah," said the grill guy, sweeping my burger and onions onto a bun and putting them on a waiting plate. "But I see him coming, going. Looks a little like Robert Taylor, only he got white hair."

"Another nut church," the plaid shirt mumbled through a mouthful of burger. "They come. They go. He opened about a year back. Before him was . . . What, Eddie?"

"Baptists," said Eddie, putting a toothpick in his mouth. "They was Baptists."

"Lot of people go to the church?" I asked. "Good burger."

"Thanks," said Eddie the grill man through the toothpick. "Not too many. Mostly old people. No Chinese. Chinese don't go for that stuff."

I finished my burger, considered ordering another one, but looked down at my gut and decided to be righteous. I dropped a half buck on the counter, pulled out my notebook, and made a note about the expense.

"Take it easy," said Eddie.

"Only way to take it," I said, scooping in the change.

I nodded at the plaid shirt, who moved his head a little to acknowledge me, and I was back on the street heading for the church. Something in the window of a store I passed caught my eye. I tried the door. It was open. A young girl was cleaning up, getting ready to close. This was the fringe of downtown, not the heart, and this was the kind of shop men with flat noses didn't usually visit.

I calmed her down by asking how much something in the window was. She told me and I pulled the cash out of my wallet. She wrapped it and handed it to me with a smile. The second I was out the door, I heard it lock behind me.

I dropped the package on the floor of the front seat of the Crosley, locked the doors again, and headed across the street for the Church of the Enlightened Patriots. A curtain on the first floor of the church moved as I crossed the street, and I caught a glimpse of one of the women who had been picketing in front of the opera—the woman who had left early. As I hit the sidewalk, the curtains parted and a man looked out at me. He was big, lean, and wearing a black suit with a white turn-around collar. His hair was bushy and white, and he smiled a confident smile he made sure I could see.

6

T he door of the Church of the Enlightened Patriots was open before I hit the top wooden step. The Reverend Adam Souvaine stood inside, hands folded in front of him, smooth face beaming at me. His eyes were green and wide, and his white mane of hair looked as if belonged on an older man, or a show horse. Behind him on the wall was an orange cross about the size of Mickey Rooney.

"Mr. Peters," he said, voice deep and steady. "Welcome to our church."

His hand was out. I took it. Firm grip. Palm and fingers hard. Behind him I could see into the small entryway.

"Reverend Souvaine," I answered.

"Please come in," he said, letting go of my hand.

The door closed behind me. Standing behind it was a man about my height but a hundred pounds heavier. The man's face was round and dark, black hair combed back. He wore a gray suit with a white turtleneck sweater. He looked like a turtle—hard, cold, slow, and determined. He also looked as if he didn't like me. I hoped it was the look he greeted all converts with.

"Mr. Ortiz is deacon of our congregation," Souvaine said, beaming at the medicine ball of a man blocking the door.

"He must give a mean sermon," I said.

"Mr. Ortiz functions best as collector of tithes, tender of the meager possessions of our church, recruiter for committees and causes. You will not believe it, Mr. Peters, but our Mr. Ortiz has had a number of careers, including that of professional wrestler, and not so long ago was a criminal in his native country. Mr. Ortiz has done some things in his day which God had difficulty forgiving, but Mr. Ortiz's sincere contrition and genuine repentance have earned him forgiveness."

A python ready to strike but kept in check by the soothing voice of his trainer, Mr. Ortiz's expression did not change. At no time in those few moments did I recognize anything on that dark, round, leathery face that resembled repentance or contrition.

"Let's continue our visit in the sanctuary," Souvaine said, taking my arm and guiding me out of the small wooden entryway and toward a room to the left. Deacon Ortiz entered the room behind us and closed the door.

The sanctuary was nothing special—an uncluttered desk and chair in the corner away from the windows, a black leather sofa, and two matching chairs with little round black buttons all over them. Jammed but neat book shelves covered the long walls. The wall behind the desk held a large, not very good painting of Jesus Christ, flanked by an equally bad painting of George Washington on the right and a much worse painting of Abraham Lincoln on the left. Below the painting of Christ was a photograph of a sober-looking man with a bushy black mustache and a collar that dug into his double chin.

"Who's the guy on the bottom?" I asked.

"That," said Souvaine, looking at the photograph of the uncomfortable man with reverence, "is J. Minor Frank, departed husband of our major benefactor, Mrs. Bertha Frank. This room," he said, with a wave of his right hand as he sat on the sofa, "is the J. Minor Frank Sanctuary. Please sit down."

I sat in one of the leather chairs. It squooshed as I sat.

"Is there anything I can get for you before we begin?" Souvaine asked smoothly. "I've asked for some lemonade."

"You can have Mr. Ortiz take a seat or lean against the wall or stand somewhere I can see him," I said.

Souvaine chuckled, amused by unfounded suspicions.

"Mr. Ortiz," he said. "Please take a seat at my side."

Ortiz looked at me as he moved next to Souvaine and sat straight on the edge of the sofa, both feet firmly on the ground.

"Thanks," I said.

"Now that we are comfortable," said Souvaine. "I assume you have some questions you would like answered. I will be happy to oblige. In fact, it is my obligation to the church and God to respond to all honest inquiry."

"How did you know my name?" I asked.

"I suppose you would not believe it if I told you God gave me your name in a vision," Souvaine said.

"I would not."

"And you would be correct." Souvaine laughed, looking at Ortiz. "I'm trying to find Mr. Ortiz's sense of humor. It is buried deeply by misfortune."

"Do I get fifty bucks if I make him laugh?"

Souvaine laughed again. "I'm afraid I cannot spend our Lord's money in such a manner," he said. "When Mr. Ortiz and God are ready, Mr. Ortiz will laugh." He looked at Mr. Ortiz with satisfaction. Mr. Ortiz continued to look at me.

"Your automobile," said Souvaine. "We simply had one of our parishioners who is employed by the local government make a call to the State Automobile License Bureau. We knew your name and the fact that you are a private investigator before you left the Opera building."

Someone knocked at the door and Souvaine called for

whoever it was to enter. In came the old lady who had spotted me from the window. She was carrying a tray, which she placed on a table in front of us.

"Bertha," said Souvaine. "How thoughtful of you. And of the kitchen ladies."

Bertha straightened up and looked at me. She wasn't sure what her feelings should be. I confused her even further.

"You're J. Minor's widow, aren't you?" I asked, reaching for something that might be lemonade. There were two other lemonades on the tray. When Souvaine reached for the one in front of him, I put mine back on the tray and took his. He shook his head and accepted the trade.

"I am," Bertha said.

"Is that the best picture you have of J. Minor?" I asked, turning to look at the uncomfortable man.

"My departed was fond of that photograph," she said, beaming at the photograph through her thick glasses. "I think he looks very stately."

"I think he looks like a man with constipation," I said.

"Mr. Peters," Souvaine said with just a touch of what might have been warning. "Is it necessary to insult the dead?"

"No," I said, "but Puccini is dead, too. Your people, including the widow Bertha, are standing in front of the Opera insulting him all day."

"He did suffer from constipation," Bertha said.

"Puccini?" I asked, surprised.

"No," said Bertha, flustered. "J. Minor suffered from constipation."

"You have a picture somewhere where he looks less in eternal pain?" I tried.

"Mr. Peters, I must . . ." Souvaine said gently.

"Only the one at the beach in his bathing suit with Errol and Faye on my birthday," said Bertha eagerly. "I think I could find it. Would that be acceptable, Reverend?"

"If it is your will and that of God," he said, turning to Bertha and taking her hands in his as he stood. "If God doesn't mind

J. Minor Frank being witnessed cavorting on the beach in his briefs, then I certainly do not mind. It is between you and God."

"I don't think I'll do it," she said, looking down at me. I sipped my lemonade and shrugged.

"Good lemonade," I said.

Souvaine ushered Bertha to the door while I toasted Deacon Ortiz, who watched me without taking his drink. When Bertha was safely out, Souvaine went back to his couch and smiled, showing perfect white teeth.

"You are good," Souvaine said.

"Not as good as you," I said. "At least at this kind of game. I play other games better."

"Our Mr. Ortiz in his youth played many games," Souvaine said, patting Ortiz's ample leg. "I think he is capable of playing them again. Is there anything else you wish to alter in the sanctuary?"

"Those paintings," I said. "Bertha must have done them."

"No."

"Then whoever sold them to you took you for a ride."

"You don't like our Jesus," he said sadly. "Or our Washington or Lincoln. You have no empathy for the heartfelt primitive artist."

I leaned forward. "You got junk on your wall, Rev," I whispered. "What do you think?"

"Mr. Ortiz painted those pictures," the Reverend whispered back.

"A man of many talents. Let's get down to business," I said.

Mr. Ortiz took his lemonade and drank it down in two gulps.

Souvaine leaned back and examined the backs of his hands before he spoke.

"Gladly," he said. "This nation was founded under God, trusting in God. It is part of our heritage. The principle of separation of Church and State is not possible. It is neither possible nor right. God does not forsake any part of his dominion. There are conflicting forces in our nation. There is a new burst of religious understanding. Do you know what the *New York Times'* best-selling novels are this week?"

"*Mother Finds a Baby* by Gypsy Rose Lee and *Love's Lovely Counterfeit* by James M. Cain," I guessed.

"*The Robe* and *The Song of Bernadette*," Souvaine countered triumphantly. "This nation has not forsaken its Christian foundations."

I wasn't sure that religious fervor accounted for the popularity of best-sellers, but Souvaine was into a sermon now, pacing the floor.

"But you are right, too, Mr. Peters. There are godless books, godless candidates. The Japanese are a godless race. To allow the presentation of a play which sympathizes with a Japanese harlot and makes a Christian American naval officer seem heartless would be to play into the hands of the enemy. And let us be clear about this. Japan is not only the enemy of the United States but the enemy of our God—for God and the United States must remain inseparable."

"Whose God?" I asked.

"There is but one true God," he said, reaching into his pocket and pulling out a clean, ironed handkerchief to wipe his brow and palms.

"You know who killed the plasterer?" I asked.

Souvaine looked at me, disoriented.

"Plasterer," I repeated. "Or who tried to strangle Lorna Bartholomew this afternoon . . . or plant an ax in my chest?"

"No."

"Might it have been God?" I tried, looking at Mr. Ortiz, who had put his lemonade glass back on the tray to give me his undivided attention.

"God does not condone murder or violence except to protect the . . ." he began and then stopped. "I do not know who did such things. I am not at all sure that I believe such things have been done. It is my understanding that the plasterer fell."

"Maybe." I said. "Have you got a live wire in the pews? Someone who might decide to give God a little help?"

"No one," Souvaine said, with righteous indignation. "None in my congregation."

"How about Mr. Ortiz?" I said, looking at the deacon. No reaction.

"Absurd," said Souvaine. "I'm afraid you see the righteousness of our cause and are—with Satan's help, whether you know it or not—trying to discredit us. It shall not be, Mr. Peters. Know you that it shall not be."

"I think I'll be going," I said, getting up.

Ortiz got up with me.

"I think that would be best," said Souvaine. "I'm sorry I have been unable to convince you of my sincerity. You receive the truth from me, Mr. Peters, more than you will receive from your Stokowski."

Souvaine moved to the desk and picked up a pad of paper with neat little letters on it. The pad had been waiting there for this moment.

"Your Leopold Stokowski is a liar, a fornicator, and we mean to expose the rot in the belly of the beast," he said without looking down at the pad. "He claims to have been born in Poland. He was not. He was born in England. That accent of his is a fraud. He invented it. He tells people that he is an expert violinist. He cannot play the instrument. He has committed adultery on numerous occasions and with both married and unmarried women, including Greta Garbo."

Souvaine threw the pad down on the table.

"How say you to these charges?"

"Reverend," I said, moving toward the door. "Your sincerity's not on the line here. Your beliefs, or the ones you're selling, are. And Stokowski's life has nothing to do with it."

"We will see to it that it becomes an issue," he said.

I reached for the door. Souvaine nodded and Ortiz stepped in front of me, barring my way, arms ready at his sides.

"I will release this information with supporting evidence to the press in the morning," said Souvaine.

"Probably boost ticket sales," I said. "Between you and me and Deacon Ortiz here, tickets aren't going so well. A little publicity might spice things up. Now please ask Mr. Ortiz to step out of the way."

"If murder and assault are going on in that building," cried Souvaine, "then I point the finger at the true Judas, the company of Satan's minions who are trying to stir up rumor and tales of the violation of God's laws to draw in the unwary."

"You change your story awfully fast, Reverend," I said.

"I'll use what I must," he said.

"Ever done any acting?" I asked, looking not at Souvaine but at Ortiz, who still blocked me.

"A bit," he said, behind me.

"Tell Deacon Ortiz to move now," I said.

"I'm not finished talking to you," Souvaine said, his voice rising. "And I will thank you to respect the Lord and his humble representative by facing me when I talk to you."

Mr. Ortiz reached out with his right hand for my shoulder. Mr. Ortiz was faster than I thought, but he did not expect my right knee to come up into his groin.

"No," screamed Souvaine behind me.

Ortiz grunted, his hands moving between his legs as he bent forward. I shoved him out of the way. At least I tried to shove him. He didn't shove easily. He grabbed my shoulder. I faked a second kick to his again uncovered groin. He didn't let go, but a reflex did make him loosen his grip. I pulled away, unzipping my new jacket. I opened the door, pulled my arms out of the sleeves, and let Mr. Ortiz stagger back a step, holding an empty jacket.

"No more violence in the house of God!" Souvaine shouted.

Ortiz stumbled after me into the hallway. Bertha was standing there with a fresh pitcher of lemonade and a frightened look on her face.

"Go with the photograph of J. Minor at the beach," I said,

moving past her to the front door. Ortiz grunted behind me as I threw it open and went down the stairs. My back, never in a good mood, threatened and warned but I couldn't listen. It was raining harder now. I ran across the street to the Crosley and got the door open. I was in the seat with the door locked when Ortiz reached the car. I started the engine and smiled at him; he moved to the front of the car. My smile stayed where it was but I had no faith in it.

People were coming out of the Church of the Enlightened Patriots. I didn't look in their direction. I looked for help on the street. There wasn't any. Ortiz was now holding the Crosley up by the front bumper, the wheels clearing the ground. I put the gears in reverse and let out the clutch. The car jerked backward and Ortiz fell forward, his face banging into the hood of my car. I was going at a good clip in reverse when about fifteen people, led by the Reverend Souvaine, emerged onto the street, looking at me. Most of the people were old. Most of the old were women.

Ortiz was standing now, blood dripping from his nose, rain trickling down his face. He picked my jacket up from where he had thrown it on the street. As I made a U-turn I watched him rip the jacket in two. For the first time since I had met him, Mr. Ortiz was smiling.

I drove fast enough and far enough to feel sure no one was following me, and then I pulled over to enter the loss of one jacket in my notebook under expenses. There was a park on my left and a small hotel called the Stanyon on my right. I'd used enough gas, met enough new friends, and had enough to eat for one day. In addition, I was wet. I reached behind the seat and pulled out my battered suitcase. I considered leaving the package I had bought in the car, but decided against it.

There were no people in the lobby, just purple chairs with curlicued wooden legs. Behind the registration desk a woman with gray-brown hair lacquered back who looked a little like Rosalind Russell was going through a pile of cards. She looked up at me as I approached and gave me a no-nonsense "Can I help you?"

"A room," I said, putting my suitcase on the counter.

"You have a reservation?" she asked, still sorting her cards.

"No," I said. "I've got money and a bad back."

"Veteran?" she asked.

"Of many wars," I said. "You always ask if your patrons have war records?"

"No," she admitted, putting her cards down. "I've just had a bad day. I'm sorry. How many nights will you be with us?"

"Probably just one. I don't know," I said. "I'll take it a day at a time."

"That seems to be best nowadays," she said, handing me the registration book. I took it and wrote in my name and address.

"Eight dollars a night," she said.

I pulled out a ten-dollar bill and placed it on the counter. She took it, gave me change, and handed me a key.

"Room twenty-one, up the stairs," she said.

I picked up my suitcase and headed up the stairs just off the desk. When I glanced down at her, the woman was staring at the hotel entrance as if another customer had come in after me. But there was no one there.

The room was small, clean, and had a bathroom with a good-size tub. I got undressed, inspected my scars, and turned on the radio. Mary Martin sang me a song, asked me to drink Royal Crown Cola, and told me to buy war bonds and stamps today. I turned the volume up and listened to "Abie's Irish Rose" on the Blue Network while I soaked in a hot tub.

I was dozing when the phone rang. I got out dripping, wrapped a towel around myself, turned down the radio, and picked up the phone.

"Mr. Peters? It's Mrs. Allen on the desk. One of the guests has asked that you turn down your radio. And you left a package on the desk. Would you like me to have it brought up to you?"

"Radio's off," I said. "Can I ask you a question?"

"Yes."

"Are you all right?"

"I just found out my husband is missing in the Pacific," she said. "Shall I send the package up?"

"No," I said. "Open it."

"Open . . . ? I don't think . . ."

"Please. It's safe."

I could hear the sound of crinkling paper as she fished the small box out of the bag. Then I could hear the box open.

"It's a hat," she said.

"Basque beret," I said. "I sell them. Please accept it as a gift from the company. If anyone asks where you got it, tell them. The tag is inside the hat."

"I can't . . ."

"Gift from a satisfied customer," I said. "I won't turn the radio on again. I hope your husband is okay."

"Thank you. Good night."

The beret had been for Vera. I could get her something else.

I went to bed. Sometime later I heard a knock at the door. When I opened it my old friend Koko the Clown was standing there in a Basque beret. He had a package in his hand. He handed it to me, but it was a ghost package. I couldn't hold it. It slipped through my hands, had no substance. As I bent to pick it up, Koko waved and into my room poured laughing people. It was a surprise party for me. Bertha Minor carried a tray with a gigantic pitcher of lemonade. Koko drank it and turned yellow. Ortiz held out two closed fists and asked me to choose. I picked the right. He turned his palm up and opened it. There were three bloody teeth. Souvaine danced in with Lorna Bartholomew, whose neck was painted blood red. Raymond Griffith arrived in neatly pressed overalls and a bright neon blue tie. He was pulling a wagon full of tools. Koko and Raymond handed out the tools, and the people in the room began to bang them together to make music. Stokowski, wearing only his underwear, arrived with a violin and began to play after giving me a wink. John Lundeen came out of the bathroom, a towel around his ample waist. He looked as if he were singing, but no sounds were coming from his mouth. I tried to tell them all to be quiet, that Mrs. Allen's husband was dead.

And then the door flew open and everyone went quiet. He was standing there, a figure draped in a black cape, wearing a black wide-brimmed hat and a white mask that covered the top half of his face. He swept into the room, cape billowing, showing a red lining.

The Phantom beckoned to me with a white-gloved right hand. I moved toward him. I was frightened, but when I was close enough I reached up quickly and pulled the mask off. The Phantom was my father. But he shook his head no and another mask appeared. I took that one off and the Phantom was my brother Phil. Another mask. This time the Phantom was me, and this scared the hell out of me. I woke up.

I started to reach for my father's watch and remembered that it wouldn't tell me the time. I picked it up anyway. The sun was up so I called the desk to ask for the time. Mrs. Allen didn't answer. The guy said she had left for the day.

"Was she wearing a little beret?" I asked.

"I . . . yes," he said. "I think so."

"What time is it?"

"Five minutes after eight."

I was shaved, dressed, and out of the hotel ten minutes later, wearing a slightly wrinkled white shirt and the same pants I had worn the day before. Time was wasting. I had an opera to save.

7

I recognized the car as soon as I turned the corner and saw the Opera building. It was Gunther Wherthman's black Daimler. Gunther had never fully explained to me how the car had come into his possession. It was simply there one morning, a specially modified model with raised pedals and seat to accommodate his size. The car, he said, was a gift he had been unable to refuse. And that was all he had ever been willing to say.

I parked behind the Daimler, got out and locked the door. Shelly Minck was engaged in conversation with the pickets from the Church of the Enlightened Patriots. There were five of them this morning. All of them were old. Sloane and Cynthia were among them. Bertha was missing. I'd half-expected Ortiz.

Some of the workers had paused on their way into the building to watch the show. Part of the show was the heavy-set bald man with the muscular neck who stood silently, almost in a trance, on the second step, watching Shelly argue with the pickets. But Jeremy Butler would have been of only minor interest if the man standing next to him had been more than three feet tall. Jeremy was wearing a white shirt and a tan windbreaker. Gunther, as always, wore a three-piece suit and a perfectly pressed tie.

Gunther was the first to see me. He touched Jeremy's sleeve and Jeremy awoke from his reverie. I joined them on the steps, shook their hands. Their grips were about the same in intensity. Jeremy, the former wrestler, was careful to control his shake, to keep it firm but gentle. Gunther wanted to demonstrate that there was a man inside the little body.

"I don't want to appear ungrateful," I said, "but what is Shelly doing here?"

"Ellis couldn't get away," said Jeremy. "Albers and Gray were not in their office. Stowell and Warren don't like San Francisco. Dr. Minck heard me calling them and volunteered. I found it impossible to dissuade him."

"We'll live with it. Politics or religion?" I asked, nodding at Shelly, who was arguing with all the pickets at once.

"Teeth," said Jeremy.

"Thanks for coming," I said. "How was the drive?"

"Without notable incident," said Gunther. "If possible, however, on the return I would prefer if Dr. Minck would travel with you."

"What'd you do with Dash?"

"Your cat," said Gunther, "is under the protection of Mrs. Plaut, who pledged to respect his needs and dignity."

I was tempted to say that Dash might well be in mortal danger if he had a sudden taste for canary. Instead, I thanked Gunther and turned to Jeremy.

"Alice?" I asked.

"Alice is doing well. She may have twins."

"Twins?"

I tried to imagine two little Jeremys or two Alices . . . or one of each.

"I'll get Shelly," I said, moving toward the little crowd.

". . . look ridiculous," Shelly was saying. He was wearing a wrinkled and food-stained plaid sport jacket over a purple short-sleeved pullover shirt. His pants were pulled up to his stomach.

"Toby," he said, seeing me. "I'm glad you came. I'm trying to explain something to these people here. You, open your mouth."

He was talking to Sloane, who seemed completely confused by this cigar-chomping man who kept pushing his thick glasses back on his nose. Sloane started to protest.

"Will you just do it?" Shelly said irritably. "I'm trying to make a point here. God, Toby, these people . . . Okay. Okay. That's fine. Look at those dentures. They look real to you?"

A few of the picketers looked at Sloane's teeth. One woman shook her head somberly.

"See. See there," said Shelly triumphantly. "What'd I tell you? You old people need false teeth that look like teeth, not like false teeth. And you need false teeth that don't smell. Any of you have dogs? You know what a dog's breath smells like?"

"Shelly," I said. "We've got to go."

"A second, Toby," he whispered, touching my arm and adjusting his cigar and glasses. "I'm doing missionary work here. You can close your mouth now," he said to Sloane, who closed his mouth. "I'm going to give each of you a card." Shelly pulled a stack of crunched business cards from his jacket pocket and began to hand them out. "You write to me and order, first, my Minck Mouth-So-Sweet Powders. You mix them with water, cola, Green River, Squirt, whatever, then gargle with it and drink it. Made especially for old guys with dentures. And if you want a set of dentures that look like real teeth instead of discolored fence posts, make an appointment with my secretary and plan a trip to Los Angeles."

"God doesn't care about such things," said a bent-over old man holding a picket sign that read: JAPANESE SOLDIERS KILL BABIES. IS THAT SOMETHING TO SING ABOUT?

"God likes bad breath?" Shelly asked, removing his cigar and pointing it at the man. "God likes silly-looking false teeth?

God sent you here to carry those signs and act like jerks, and he sent me to see to it that you look like human beings and don't smell like cocker spaniels. Think about it."

Shelly moved to the man who had complained and pulled the calling card out of his hand.

"Let's go, Shel," I said, taking his arm.

"All right, all right."

"Mouth-So-Sweet Powder?" I asked.

"Buy some bottles, slap a few labels on, mix some stuff up," he said.

"Make an appointment with your secretary?" I went on.

"I use a high voice when I answer the phone," he explained.

We moved up the steps toward Jeremy and Gunther.

"You're trying to sell those people the same stuff you're working on for dog breath, aren't you?" I whispered.

"Works just as well on people," he said, putting on a false smile and waving back at the picketers. "I'll be careful with it. I haven't really got it fully developed yet."

The show was over. The workers were heading into the building or setting up on the steps. We entered the lobby. It looked further along today, but that might have been either my imagination or better lighting.

We ducked under some scaffolding and headed for the marble stairway.

"Nice place," Shelly said. "What time's the next decapitation?"

"Samuel Varney Keel," said Gunther. "This is distinctly his work. He could never decide in which century he wished to place his faith. His buildings have the rococo design of the sixteenth century, poorly blended with museum memories of Greek and Roman statuary. There, up there, even an bit of ersatz ancient Egypt. And his edifices are pocked with hidden chambers and passages drawn from English Gothic tales."

"Interesting," I said as we hit the top of the stairs where we had found Lorna Bartholomew crying the day before.

"Keel died quite mad," said Gunther. "I translated a brochure on San Francisco architects. This is how I know such things."

"Looks okay to me," Shelly said. "Little dark. Some nice paintings of girls in the woods, or movie posters, could brighten it up."

"What do you think, Jeremy?" I asked as we paused in front of Lundeen's office.

"There is an aura of death," said Jeremy. "I felt it outside. I feel it more strongly in here. It reminds me of the House of Usher."

"That would probably have pleased Mr. Keel," said Gunther.

Shelly looked as if he were going to say something but decided to keep it to himself. I knocked and Lundeen sang for us to enter.

Long sheets of paper covered the floor, desk, and table. Lundeen stood over the table looking down, a handkerchief in his hand to dry his palms. Gwen was asleep in an overstuffed chair in a corner, a sheet of paper on her lap, her mouth open.

Lundeen looked at the four of us. His jaw dropped. He touched his stubbly face, closed his mouth, and pulled himself together.

"My colleagues," I said, and introduced everyone. Lundeen was quite an actor. He smiled politely and shook each hand.

"Welcome, gentlemen," he said. "Mr. Peters, Gwen and I have spent the night going over the statements you asked us to obtain. Gwen will put it all together after she has some rest. But as far as we can tell, everyone from the custodial staff to me and the Maestro were seen either when the plasterer was being killed or when Lorna and you were attacked. It must have been someone from the outside."

"I would like to examine these reports, if I may," said Gunther.

"Yes, of course," Lundeen conceded.

Shelly had wandered over to the sleeping Gwen. "Good teeth on this girl," he said appreciatively, coming back to us. "Slight overbite."

"What now?" asked Lundeen. "Vera, Marty Passacaglia, the Maestro, and the orchestra will be here in the next few minutes. What do we . . . ?"

"My colleagues are experienced at this kind of thing," I said, pretending to look at one of the sheets of paper.

Lundeen rubbed his eyes and looked at us with disbelief.

"Got some questions," I said, looking up. "Last night I ran into the Reverend Souvaine, the guy behind the picketers. He said he's going to drop a publicity bomb today, that he has proof Stokowski is a liar—that he isn't Polish, that he can't play the violin—that he has been fooling around with women for years."

"All true," said Lundeen with a sigh, standing up to straighten his shirt front. "The Maestro is a storyteller and a mass of contradictions. He values his privacy but enjoys adulation. He changes his biography. His accent is a fraud, a mixture of precise English and playful European pronunciations. He is an accomplished organist, a virtuoso. There is no reason for him to claim the violin. Yet he does so. His exploits with women are legendary in the business. Your Reverend . . ."

". . . Souvaine," I said.

". . . will get a few lines in the paper, but there is nothing the community does not know about the Maestro," Lundeen concluded. "Now, if you don't mind, I'd like to change my shirt, shave, and try to look presentable. The Maestro doesn't like slovenliness. You might want to get your people down to the lobby before he arrives."

Lundeen moved toward a door in the right wall, opened it, and disappeared.

"I am able to confirm what Mr. Lundeen has said about Leopold Stokowski," said Gunther. "The discrepancies have been evident for a long time."

Gwen sat up suddenly and found herself looking at Shelly. She stifled a scream, her eyes searching for help. She saw

Gunther and then Jeremy. Her mouth opened and her eyes found me.

"Good morning," I said.

"Bad dream," she whispered hoarsely, trying to sit up.

Gunther moved to help her.

"Thank you," she said. "Mr. Lundeen . . . ?"

"Shaving," I said.

"He told you what we found? Or failed to find?"

"Perhaps you would not mind summarizing your information for me," said Gunther.

Gwen touched her hair and sat up.

"Okay, Gunther, you stay here and work on the statements," I said. "If we have anything to add, we'll bring it to you. You keep an eye on Gwen."

"Of course," he said.

Jeremy, Shelly, and I left the room.

We made it to the lobby just in time. Members of the orchestra were coming in, carrying instruments, talking, pointing out grotesque designs and rococo corners. Behind them, a light coat over his shoulders, came Stokowski, with Lorna and Miguelito at his side. Under his coat Stokowski wore a gray suit with a black shirt and white tie. He looked like a king going to a costume ball dressed like a movie gangster. He looked up at me as he entered.

"Ah, my detective," he said. "What have you discovered?"

"Everyone has an alibi for everything," I said.

"As is always true in detective fiction," he said.

I introduced Shelly and Jeremy. Stokowski shook their hands.

"I am an admirer of your work," Jeremy said.

Stokowski nodded, having heard it before, the polite response of someone who meets a celebrity.

"Exclusively of my work?" he asked with a wry smile.

"No," said Jeremy. "Not exclusively. I enjoy the New York Philharmonic, though I find them a bit too formal under Bruno Walter, except when they are doing Beethoven. The London

Philharmonic under Sir Thomas Beecham is suited for Debussy, although not for the more intense composers, and while Felix Weingartner and the London Symphony have a remarkable range, they have, in my opinion, no singular identity or strength. Admittedly, my familiarity with these orchestras is through recordings, the quality of which varies greatly. Your recordings, however, are consistently of the highest quality. In addition, I find your dedication to modern composers and your willingness to deal with the most difficult classics admirable. In my opinion, only your friend Artur Rodzinski, with the Cleveland Orchestra, approaches your virtuosity."

Stokowski had stopped and was regarding the large bear-like bald man in front of him.

"You are a musician?" he asked.

"A poet," Jeremy said.

"Used to wrestle," said Shelly. "Pro. Broke Tiger Daniels' arm in Pittsburgh in 1930."

Stokowski looked at Jeremy and smiled. "I look forward to talking with you further."

He pulled the coat around his shoulders and hurried into the building.

"Are you all right?" I asked Lorna. She wore a scarf around her neck. I had a flash image of her red neck from my dream.

"No," she said, looking around at the workmen and up the stairway. "And Miguelito couldn't sleep. He was traumatized."

"Shelly, will you accompany Miss Bartholomew while she is in the building?" I said.

"Sure," said Shelly, taking Lorna's arm. Miguelito took a snap in his direction and Shelly let go.

We heard his voice as he led her away: "Little fellow has a nice smile there, but there's just a slight underbite, and his teeth need cleaning."

"Stay with Stokowski," I told Jeremy.

Jeremy nodded and moved silently toward the auditorium.

Vera came in about two minutes later, but she wasn't alone.

A tall blond man was laughing at her side. She was smiling. The man wasn't just tall. He was also muscular and handsome. Then Vera spotted me and the smile disappeared.

The two of them moved toward me.

"I'm sorry about last night," she said. "Lorna's much better."

"I saw her," I said. "Inside. Let's try for those carrot sandwiches tonight."

"Who is this?" asked the man with Vera.

"I'm sorry," Vera said, clearly flustered. "This is Mr. Peters, the detective Maestro Stokowski has hired. Toby, this is Martin Passacaglia."

I put out my hand. Passacaglia took it and gave it his best. He was about fifteen years younger than me and in good shape, but it was body-building shape, not scar tissue shape. I let him squeeze.

"Good to meet you, Peters," he said. His voice sang—I liked that voice, reminded me of Robert Preston. "Let's get inside, Vera. Stoki will be waiting," he added.

"Go ahead, Martin," she said. "I'll be with you in a minute."

"Nice dress," I said, trying my best smile. The dress was nice—yellow, plenty of room on top to breathe, with just enough flesh showing in the V-cut of the neck.

"Peters," said Passacaglia sweetly, trying to lead Vera away. "We have work to do, and so have you."

I reached over and put my hand on the hand holding Vera's arm.

"Go inside, Mr. Passacaglia," I said with a smile. "I've played scenes like this more than you have, and they never come out with a song. They come out with bloody noses and cracked teeth."

"You are coming dangerously close to insolence and the loss of this employment," said Passacaglia.

"What are you two fighting about?" asked Vera.

"You," I explained.

She blushed. I thought it was cute.

"I'm giving you a warning, Peters," Passacaglia hissed through perfect white teeth.

"Mr. Peters," came a voice behind us. I turned to face Lundeen. "You have been hired to protect, not attack, the company. If you inflict bodily harm to Mr. Passacaglia, you will have to collect your fee from the Phantom."

Passacaglia took this moment to sneer and make his exit. Vera followed him, giving me a quick, small wave of her hand.

"The man can't act," said Lundeen with a sigh. "Best we could get, however. And he can sing. He is obnoxious, I grant you, but we do need him for this opera."

"He didn't seem to be afraid of the Phantom," I said.

"Martin is far too stupid to be afraid," said Lundeen, looking into the theater lobby hallway into which Vera and Martin had disappeared. "He has been killed in so many operas that he thinks he is immortal. A strange malady peculiar to tenors and fools."

A pair of women in work clothes, carrying paint buckets, moved quickly past us. Some paint sloshed out of one of their cans and Lundeen jumped back.

"What happened to professional pride?" he asked, loud enough for the two women to hear. They kept walking. He turned to me. He had something to say. We stood looking at each other.

"Think I should take in Mt. Lassen while I'm in town?" I asked.

"I am not impressed by your colleagues, Mr. Peters," he said, mopping his brow with his handkerchief.

"I thought we were Toby and John, drinking buddies."

"Your colleagues are . . ."

". . . cleverly disguised," I said. "Gunther is trained in the use of Swiss weaponry and explosives. He's taller than he looks. And Shelly is a hand-to-hand combat expert who lulls his opponents into complacency with his pretense of being a buffoon. Jeremy, I must admit, is along for the ride. Smart man, but can't stand the sight of blood."

"Amusing," said Lundeen.

"I'll make a deal with you, John," I said. "I don't think much of Passacaglia. You send him home and I'll let you pick out one of my men to send home."

Lundeen sighed deeply. "I've told you I need Martin."

"And I need my team."

"I give up," he said dramatically, putting his handkerchief back in his pocket, tears moistening his eyes. "Keep your clowns. You are the Maestro's choice. It will be his responsibility. I wash my hands of it all. My life is total misery. I leave myself in the hands of the gods."

"Very convincing, John," I said. "That from an opera?"

The look of despair suddenly left Lundeen's face. "I think so," he said, "but I'll be damned if I can remember which one. Toby, can I be honest?"

"Try," I said.

"Leave Vera alone and please concentrate on the job. I need you. We need you."

I was going to argue, but he was right. I nodded. He clapped a heavy hand on my shoulder.

"I was really convincing, eh?" he said, guiding me toward the auditorium.

"Beautiful performance," I said.

"Acting, that's a talent you never lose," he said. "Martin is safe. He's never had the talent. I'm invigorated. A few hours' sleep and I'll be ready to go out to lunches and sell tickets to the tone deaf and ancient who think of opera as a deadly responsibility. There are but a few, a precious few, in this country who really appreciate the art. I remember . . ."

There was a sudden noise, as if a bomb had exploded through the ceiling. Lundeen looked at me for an opinion. I didn't have one. I left him and ran down the hall toward the auditorium. I could hear him panting after me.

As I ran through the rear door toward the stage, the entire orchestra, Stokowski, Vera, and Martin Passacaglia were looking up the aisle toward me. Shelly was turned in his seat in the front row, and Jeremy was running up the aisle in my direction. A man-sized grasshopper shape lay just in front of me. I reached it at the same time as Jeremy. Lundeen came up behind me and stopped suddenly.

"It fell from there," Jeremy said, pointing upward.

There was nothing up there but a darkened balcony. I considered running like hell up to the balcony, but there was no hurry. I turned instead to the twisted mass that had crushed an aisle seat and lay in front of me.

"What is it?" called Stokowski from the stage.

"A projector," Lundeen called back. "A rusty old movie projector."

"Lorna!" Vera cried.

There was a movement to my right and Lorna Bartholomew sat up between the seats, her eyes open wide, blood on her forehead.

". . . tried again," she whimpered, looking at Lundeen.

Lundeen moved to help her.

"Don't you touch me! Why is he trying to kill me?" she wailed. "Where is Miguelito?"

Vera was hurrying down the aisle, followed by Passacaglia. Shelly waddled behind them, Miguelito yapping in his arms.

"Lorna!" Vera cried again.

"Is she hurt?" Stokowski called as he strode toward us.

"No," said Lundeen. "Just frightened."

"I quit," screamed Lorna. "I'm not dying for an opera."

She put out her arms for the dog, and Shelly let the animal leap to her. The impact almost knocked her over.

"A good symphony, perhaps," said Stokowski, "but I agree with you: not for an opera."

Lorna looked at him as if he were mad and saw a small mischievous smile on the Maestro's face.

Stokowski touched the shoulder of a woman with glasses who had moved up the aisle carrying a flute. She handed the flute to Lundeen and put her arm around Lorna.

"Let's take her up to my office," Lundeen said.

"No," Lorna said, suddenly calm, suddenly sober. "I wish to leave this building. I wish never to return to this building. I wish to live. Some may think I have little to live for, but that is not my view. The person responsible for this will regret it."

The woman who had handed Lundeen her flute helped Vera guide Lorna and her dog into the aisle and past the twisted mass of the projector.

"Am I being calm, Maestro?" Lorna asked, a trickle of blood winding down her nose and around her mouth.

"Perfectly," Stokowski assured her.

"Good," she said. "That's all I want to know."

And she was ushered out the door and into the lobby.

"Mr. Peters," Stokowski said, "I'm going to call a short break and then have the orchestra continue to rehearse with the cast. Do you think you and your fellows can keep death at bay long enough to let us get through the first act?"

Passacaglia grinned over Stokowski's shoulder.

"Jeremy, Shelly, get every light in this place on and sit on the stage with your eyes open," I said.

Jeremy nodded.

"She said she had to go to the toilet, Toby," Shelly whimpered. He turned to Stokowski. "She gave me the dog. I couldn't follow her into the toilet, could I?"

"You could," Stokowski said, "but I wouldn't advise it."

"See," said Shelly. "Even Toscanini says I couldn't help it."

The place went dead. Eyes turned to the Maestro. He shook his head, turned his back, and moved back toward the stage.

"Five minutes, ladies and gentlemen," he said softly.

"What did I say?" whined Shelly, sensing blunder, a sensation familiar to him. "I said something?"

"Jeremy will explain," I said. "I'm going to find Raymond."

"Raymond?" asked Shelly. "Who the hell is Raymond?"

"The man who knows where everything is around here," I said, moving toward the exit. "Might know something about projectors."

8

Finding Raymond left me tired, dirty, and a little confused. I got lost in dusty corridors and dead ends. Then I borrowed a flashlight from a reluctant painter. Raymond had said something about living in the tower. There were five towers in the Opera. All of them were up wooden stairways.

The first stairway I tried was at the end of a narrow corridor. The walls were decorated with blue and white plaster drapes that wouldn't have fooled Shelly with his glasses off, even if there weren't chunks gouged out of the plaster. Between the plaster drapes were paintings of overstuffed horses and guys dressed in red uniforms, little hats, and boots. Shelly would have liked the horses. They all had big teeth and looked as if they were familiar with bad breath. The corridor looked like the lobby of the Chinese Theater in L.A. in the middle of a renovation.

The stairway was rotten, but I made it to the top and found a padlocked room. The lock was rusty. I pulled at it and it came off. It took two kicks to get the door open wide enough for me to get in.

Enough light got through the dirty windows to show me that someone back in the bad old days had used the place to entertain himself and whatever ladies he could lure to his red velvet lair. There were mirrors as high as a basketball net at angles surrounding a big square bed. The mirrors were smoked and dirty but showed the image of the bed behind their cloud cover. There were indentations in the ancient mattress, the memory of bodies, proving that sex wasn't invented in the Roaring Twenties. The couch and two chairs were covered in red velvet, and on the wall hung the portrait of a man with his hands on his hips, his long hair combed back, his head cocked to one side. He was a little on the heavy side, but he made up for it in confidence. His smile was all teeth and phony.

The second tower had fewer ghosts and no portraits. It took me a while to get there, but I finally found a hallway with statues of old men draped in stone robes. I half-expected to run into Billy Batson. The steps to this tower were in no better shape than the first one I'd tried, but the room at the top wasn't locked. It was filled with magazines—piles of magazines, magazines toppled over, magazines scattered. All covered with a layer of gray dust.

I picked up a *Popular Mechanics* from 1913 and discovered that submarines would be the most important weapon of the twentieth century and that someone was planning a cruise ship with more space inside it than Yankee Stadium. A 1905 *Police Gazette* with the cover missing had a story about how much it would cost to keep the Chinese out of the U.S.A., and suggested that it would be worth every penny. I tried one more magazine. It was *Casket and Sunnyside*, the undertakers' journal. I threw it in a corner, hoping the tower I was looking for wouldn't be the fifth one.

It wasn't.

The third tower was Raymond's. I could tell because the

stairs were not as covered with dust, and the door at the top was locked.

Music was coming from behind the door, a violin. I knocked and the music stopped. I knocked again. No answer.

"Raymond," I called. "I know you're in there."

"No you don't," he said.

"I heard you playing," I said. "And besides, you just answered me."

"You're smart. I'll give you that," he said.

"I appreciate your praise," I said. "Let me in. Someone tried to kill Lorna Bartholomew again."

I heard his steps move toward the door, and a bolt pulled.

"Why do you keep the door bolted if you've been the only one in the building for years?" I asked, stepping into the room and looking around.

"Lived a lot of years being cautious," he replied.

"Can't argue with that," I said, looking around.

The room was lighted with three fancy, turn-of-the century lamps. Two plush couches faced each other in the center of the room. Behind them was a massive four-poster bed. The walls were draped with tapestries—one a scene of men in feathered hats about to shoot a deer, another a scene of two men with feathered hats whispering while two young women stood giggling at a fountain. A violin lay on one of the couches. A phonograph, an old wind-up thing with a megaphone speaker, sat on an ornate table. The chest of drawers in the corner looked as if it had been designed for a giant with a taste for fancy wedding cakes.

"Props," he said. "Pulled 'em up here years ago. Gonna turn me in?"

"No," I said. "You play the violin."

"Play every damned instrument man invented," he said proudly. "Even the lyre. Nothing else to do. One instrument a year, night after night. Plenty of music. Plenty of instruments. And I can repair them all. Can play any tune. You name it.

Name the instrument and I'll play the song on it. Even do ragtime on a French horn."

"'Sheik of Araby' on a tuba," I said.

"Hell, I can do that," he said. "Do it sitting on a toilet."

"Projectors," I said as he looked around the room for either a toilet or a tuba or both. He stopped looking.

"Projectors," he repeated, turning to me.

"Movie projectors," I said. "One of them almost killed Miss Bartholomew."

"Couple of old Edison projectors in the balcony," he said, picking up his violin. "Can play this thing like a guitar. Listen."

He started to plunk, and I put my hand out to stop him.

"Where were you fifteen minutes ago?" I asked.

"Where? Here practicing."

"No one can be as eccentric as you pretend to be." I looked him directly in the eye.

"Son," he said, "it is not easy. I'm the harmless old coot. The character every good theater needs. If I didn't exist, they'd have to go out and cast me."

"I thought so," I said.

"Thought so, hell," Raymond said. "I'm the genuine article. Been playing this role so long I *am* it. Don't know where my act begins and ends. Danger of playing any role too long. You want my secret? I was an actor. When this place was a theater, I was an actor in the last show. Quake came and went and I stayed. Didn't have much money. Didn't plan to stay. Went out for some roles. Didn't get them. It just happened."

"Someone who knows this place has killed a man, tried to kill me and Miss Bartholomew," I said. "You're the only one who knows this place that well."

"Miss Bartholomew," he said. "Tell my old Granny. I was with the fat guy when she came screaming. Ask him."

He was right. He had come down the hall with Lundeen seconds after Lorna had come up the stairs after the Phantom . . . or someone . . . had tried to strangle her.

"Coming to you, son?" he asked.

"Yeah, but I don't give up easy."

"No man worth a brass turd would," he said.

"Cut it out, Raymond," I said.

"Told you, I can't. Lots of people have been nosing around this place since they decided to open it up again," Raymond said. "That fat guy."

"He was with you when Miss Bartholomew was attacked, remember?" I said. "Lose him and you lose your alibi."

"I see what you mean," he acknowledged, reaching a bony finger to touch an itch just under his nose. "I've spent too damn much time alone to make sense. Want a sandwich? I got Prem and stuff in an icebox."

"No, thanks," I said. "We'll be talking again."

"I'll practice up for it," said Raymond with a snaggle-toothed grin.

I was down the second step of the tower when the violin began to play ragtime behind me. I was on the way to the third step when I saw Jesus Ortiz standing in front of me.

"Lost?" I asked pleasantly.

I would have liked an answer, something to bounce off of, but the Deacon Jesus Ortiz did the one thing I would have preferred not to see. He grinned, and the grin was not pretty. His teeth were large and close to white and he looked happy. The bridge of his nose was raw from where it had met the hood of my Crosley the night before. I backed up a step. He didn't follow.

Behind me Raymond Griffith was playing a Scott Joplin version of "Anything Goes," no mean trick on a fiddle, but I really couldn't appreciate it at the time.

Ortiz was wearing a new light gray suit.

"Nice suit," I tried.

The closest sound I could equate to what Ortiz gave out was the snort of a pregnant seal I once saw in the Griffith Park Zoo.

I backed up. I was running out of back-up room. My back was to Raymond's door. I reached behind me and knocked as Jesus Ortiz, who had all the time in the world, moved—or rather, hulked—toward me, getting happier with each step. Raymond's playing grew a little less frenzied.

"What you want?" he called.

"I forgot something," I said.

"Can't stop," Raymond shouted. "The muse has got me."

There was about five feet of space between Ortiz and me, and through, above, or beyond Raymond's playing, I could have sworn Ortiz was humming.

There was no room to get past Ortiz, and Raymond was taken by the muse.

"I don't think Reverend Souvaine would want you . . ." I began, but Ortiz was shaking his head.

"He would want you to . . ." I went on.

When Ortiz was close enough to kiss my chin and for me to smell Adam's Clove on his breath, I threw a right cross to his stomach. He didn't even bother to block it. My fist hit solid concrete just above the kidney.

I threw a left toward his already tender nose. His shoulder came up and caught the blow. I came up with my right knee. He turned so the kneecap hit his thigh. I was running out of ideas.

Ortiz's right hand came up and grasped my arm. It did more than hurt.

"You got a mother?" I asked.

He shook his head no.

Raymond stopped playing and complained, "Stop the noise out there, will you? Thirty years I hear nothing but creaking and mice, and wouldn't you know it, the day I get inspired, a bunch of hooligans set up a circus on my doorstep."

"Raymond," I called to him as Ortiz's left hand came up toward my throat. "Call for help, now."

"Got no phone," Raymond bleated. "Got no phone. Got no phone. Told you that. I got nothing in here but what I got in here, and now I don't have my inspiration."

Jesus Ortiz's thick fingers now had a firm grip on my neck, and I was getting a headache. He was definitely humming, but

I didn't know the tune. He pulled my head down to him and put his mouth to my ear.

"I'm gonna pop your eyeballs," he whispered in a surprisingly high voice.

I took little comfort in the knowledge that he could talk. My head was throbbing.

"Murder," I gasped.

"Yeah," he said. "Murder *puta*."

"God will . . ." I groaned.

"God's will, *si*," he said.

I'll be truthful here. I'm not sure if Deacon Ortiz would have killed me if Jeremy hadn't appeared on the landing behind him. Maybe he was just planning to cause me great pain and murder Raymond's inspiration. But there, over the deacon's shoulder, I saw Jeremy Butler. I hadn't heard him come up the stairs.

I did hear the door behind me open and Raymond shout, "Begone!"

Ortiz did not see Jeremy, but he did see something in my eyes—hope of salvation—and he saw that my eyes were looking over his shoulder. Without letting me go, he turned. Raymond saw a bald giant moving forward, noticed that a marble slab of a man was about to strangle me, and hastily closed his door.

"I know you," Ortiz said to Jeremy.

"Wichita, 1934," said Jeremy. "Baseball park. You wrestled Man Mountain Dean in the headline."

Ortiz considered. I began to pass out.

"Butler," he said. "You wrestled my brother, Jaime. You broke Jaime's shoulder."

Jeremy ambled slowly forward and reached up toward Ortiz's left hand, which was now only vaguely visible to me as I started to pass out.

"Your brother lost control," Jeremy said. "He tried to kill me."

"He wasn't as good as me," said Jesus with a smile, giving

me a little love squeeze so I'd groan and let him know I was still alive.

"No," said Jeremy, putting his hand on Ortiz's wrist. "He wasn't."

"And you was old then," Ortiz said, looking at Jeremy's hand as it began to squeeze his wrist.

"I was old then," Jeremy admitted. "But I was not at peace, as I am now."

Ortiz was grinning widely. Raymond began to play again. Only this time the playing was madness. No tune. Just noise. Screeching noise and anger.

I knew Jeremy was getting somewhere in spite of Jesus Ortiz's grin because I felt the deacon's fingers loosen. Not much, but enough so I thought I might be approaching a breath.

"Let him go," Jeremy said softly.

Jesus shook his head no.

Jeremy's free hand came up, open-palmed and fast. It caught Ortiz on the side of the head. Ortiz didn't stagger. He did let me go. He did hiss. But he didn't step back.

"I think I'll break your shoulder, old man," he said as I slid back against Raymond's door.

My hand caught the handle. I turned it and the damned thing opened. I fell into Raymond's room and heard him shout, "Where the hell is a human being's right to priv-a-see?"

My head was a mass of pain. I looked up from the floor where I was sitting and saw Jeremy and Ortiz holding hands. They were facing each other, Jeremy's right grasping Ortiz's left and his left Ortiz's right.

"The hell with charity," cried Raymond, and started a new tune on his fiddle. It sounded a little too much like "After You've Gone."

Jeremy and Ortiz, their fingers locked, began to dance to the music. At least it looked as if they were dancing to the music. My plan was to leap to my feet, find something heavy, and crack Ortiz's skull. That was my plan, but when I tried to get up I slumped back to the floor, my head warning me of certain disaster if I dared to move.

Jeremy and Ortiz waltzed past the door, grunting, trying to keep their faces from turning red. Ortiz continued to grin. Jeremy showed nothing. Mid-tune Raymond changed to a Strauss waltz to make life easier for the dancing bears. On their next pass they fell through the door and tumbled to the floor, almost crushing me.

"I suppose," said Raymond, continuing to play, "there would be no point in asking you to leave my abode."

Jeremy hurtled across the room, crushed a fragile-looking, dirty-pink chair. He was rising slowly as Ortiz got to one knee and then lunged, landing on him and sending him tumbling backward into the old Victrola on a rickety table. The Victrola swayed. Ortiz's fingers found the flower-shaped speaker and ripped it from the machine.

"Oh, oh," groaned Raymond. "That'll do it. No more music. No more hospitality. Out you all go."

Ortiz was about to clobber Jeremy with the speaker when Raymond hit him on the neck with his fiddle. The fiddle shattered; a piece of it came twanging past my head as I got to one knee. It didn't really stop Ortiz, who was humming again, but it did distract him for a heartbeat. The heartbeat was enough for Jeremy to bring his head up sharply into Ortiz's nose.

Ortiz dropped the Victrola speaker and stepped back. His hand moved up to his nose. Blood streamed from between his fingers, but I'll be damned if he wasn't still humming. He took his hand down and looked at each of us, his face a bloody mask, his grinning teeth smeared red. Jeremy stepped forward on pieces of crushed furniture. He staggered slightly. Ortiz lunged forward again, arms out. Jeremy went down on one knee and caught the flying barrel of flesh on his shoulder.

"No point asking you not to break anything more, is there?" asked Raymond.

Jeremy had Ortiz on his shoulders now. Ortiz, who couldn't

have weighed less than 240 pounds, was grasping at his opponent's bald head in search of a forgotten hair. He threw a fist at Jeremy's back, but Jeremy slowly stood erect. Ortiz's head went down and his teeth dug into Jeremy's shoulder. A tic crossed Jeremy's mouth but he didn't pause. He hoisted Ortiz over his head and began to spin, slowly at first and then faster.

As he spun, Ortiz stopped biting and began to growl. I couldn't tell where Ortiz's blood stopped and Jeremy's began, and as they spun I couldn't tell where one man began and the other ended. They were a dizzying blur. My stomach heaved, did more than threaten. I looked around for a vase, a bucket. Nothing. The two men spun and Raymond reached down to help me up, saying, "I'm gonna take this real philosophical. New company's moving in. New company'll clean it up. Always be new shows. New sets."

Suddenly Jeremy stopped. Ortiz flew toward me and Raymond. I pulled Raymond down. Ortiz landed upside down on Raymond's sofa. The legs crunched and Ortiz lay silent.

"Jeremy," I said. "You all right?"

"I endure," Jeremy said softly, catching his breath. "Is he alive?"

I made my way to Ortiz, whose feet were dangling over the top of the sofa, his head tilted downward. His lips were moving and a humming sound was coming out. I touched him. He smiled through red teeth.

"I think his shoulder's broken," I said.

Jeremy moved forward and looked down at Ortiz.

"An irony," he said. Little beads of sweat stood out on his forehead. His clothes and cheek were covered with blood.

"Paddy wagon, funny farm cart, or ambulance?" asked Raymond, moving toward the door.

"Ambulance," I said.

"I have decided to move to quieter climes," Raymond said. And he was gone.

"Lucky you came," I said as Jeremy and I turned Ortiz so that he was in something close to a lying-down position.

"I had a message for you," he said. "You are . . ." and then he paused and stared at the wall.

"What's wrong?" I asked.

"A breeze just touched the fine hairs on the back of my hand and a voice whispered 'mortality,'" he said softly.

"I'm sorry," I said.

"It was both frightening and restful," he said.

I looked at his bloody face and bulldog neck. Jeremy Butler didn't always make a hell of a lot of sense to me.

"The message for me?" I asked.

He sighed, opened Ortiz's right eye with his thumb, examined him for further signs of life, and replied, "Miss Bartholomew asked that you come to her apartment. She says she has information you should have. She gave me her address and number."

Jeremy reached a hand into his shirt pocket. One of his fingers had been bitten by Ortiz. I could see the indentations from the deacon's teeth. I took the piece of paper.

"I think you'd best go before the police arrive," Jeremy said.

"You want to know what this was all about?" I asked, rubbing my sore neck.

"Perhaps later," he said, moving to the window. "If you think it essential that I know."

"Thanks, Jeremy," I said. "Sure you're okay?"

He turned to look at me and smiled sadly.

"Every time I have wrestled or been engaged in combat," he said, "I have been lost within the space and time of the encounter. I have been within and outside of myself. My concentration has always been complete with no sense of ego, but in this room I did not merge with my movements. I was aware that I would soon be a father. It was then that mortality touched me. I felt very much alive."

"Great," I said with enthusiasm, hoping that was the right comment.

"Go," he said. And I went.

On the way out, I found Gunther waiting for Stokowski in the lobby.

"You are injured?" he asked with concern.

"I'm all right," I said, and gave him directions up to Raymond's tower in case Raymond didn't get back. He said that the rehearsal had been cut short by Stokowski and that everyone had left except for Stokowski and Vera Tenatti. Shelly, he said, was watching outside Vera's door.

I thanked him and hurried for Vera's dressing room. Shelly was nowhere in sight. I knocked and Vera called, "Come in."

I came in and Shelly came hurtling at me from a corner, one hand holding his glasses on, the other out like a stiff-arming half-back. He missed me by a good two feet and tumbled into an open closet filled with Vera's costumes.

Vera gasped.

"Shelly," I said, helping him up. "What the hell are you doing?"

"We heard a voice," Vera said. She was standing next to her dressing table.

"A voice," Shelly agreed. "Man. Right out of the wall."

"He said," Vera began, and then shuddered. "He said, 'She will die before she sings for the Lion. I will strike within the hour.'"

"I've been hiding behind the door," said Shelly, on his feet now.

"He plans to kill me," said Vera, her eyes wide.

I moved to comfort her. She felt warm and smelled great.

"I don't think he meant you," I said. "I think he meant Lorna. I think he meant he would get her before she sings to me."

"You?" There was disbelief in her voice.

"You're no lion," said Shelly. "Besides, he's nuts. Why would he tell us he was going to kill Lorna what's-her-name? What lion?"

"My middle name is Leo," I said.

"Pretty filmsy," said Shelly, finding a piece of cigar in his pocket and lighting it.

I gave the note from Lorna to Vera.

"Call the police. Those two cops who were here, Preston and Nighttime . . ."

". . . Sunset," she corrected.

"Call them and send them to Lorna's. I'll meet them there."

I didn't think about it. I just gave Vera a kiss. It seemed the right thing to do and the right time to do it. She kissed back. Middle of Act Two. Knight off to war—Wish me luck, babe. And I was off.

Gunther wasn't in the lobby. I ran out into the street, not knowing where I was going. The ancient pickets, about a dozen of them, were there, and in their midst, in a white suit that outdid the sunshine, was the Reverend Adam Souvaine. He looked up at me as I came down the steps and barely flinched. He kept talking. I skipped past a woman in overalls who was plastering a top step and went down two by two, heading for my Crosley.

Souvaine popped out of the crowd and beat me to my car.

"Did you see Deacon Ortiz within?" he asked softly.

"We had a nice chat," I said. "Step out of the way."

"We have decided to forgive you for your un-Christian behavior of last night," Souvaine said, brushing back his stately white mane and waving to his seniors a few dozen yards away.

"Deacon Ortiz was very forgiving," I said, "but he was so elated at my sudden conversion that he fell over a lion."

"Cryptic," said Souvaine. "You have a gift for the parable."

"Get your ass away from my car or you're dog meat," I snarled, reaching for the handle.

Souvaine smiled sweetly, put his hands up, and moved away from the Crosley.

"I'm sure that if you let yourself listen to us, you'd find our cause just," he said. "Let me help you. Let us help you."

"Okay," I said, getting into the Crosley and opening the window. "How do I get to Las Lindas Road?"

"You are within a mile of it," he said with a put-upon smile. "Back that way three blocks and then right for another four or five blocks."

"Thanks," I said, turning the ignition key. "You don't seem particularly concerned about Deacon Ortiz and the lion."

"The Lord will do what the Lord will do," he said.

As I turned the car around, I heard the wail of an ambulance heading toward the Opera.

9

I picked up an armed forces' relay of one of last summer's Yankees–White Sox games on the radio. I didn't remember the game. I urged the Crosley forward and tried not to think. DiMaggio hit a double to drive in two runs in the eighth, and the announcer was going wild.

I got lost, or the Reverend Souvaine had given me bum directions.

I drove through streets that smelled of bodies, gasoline, and Mexican food. If your nose was good, you could also smell the grease of frying kielbasa. The smell seemed right for the people of the street, mostly dark-skinned and Latin but with a few older, round pink-white faces and heavy bodies. I passed stores with signs in Polish, including Slotvony's Meat Shop, which sported a white sign in crayon announcing that blood soup was on sale today.

Finally, I blundered onto Las Lindas, spotted the address, and was looking for a place to park when a figure staggered out in front of my Crosley. I was going slow, the car was small, and his brain was parked on another planet or he would have

97

been dead when I hit him. I pulled in next to a fire plug, pulled my .38 out of the glove compartment, stuck it in my pocket, got out, and moved over to the guy I had hit.

"You okay?" I asked, helping him up.

He smelled fragrant, but he was thin and easy to lift.

"I'm disoriented," the guy said.

"I know how you feel," I said, fishing into my pocket, one-handing my wallet and pulling out a bill. It was a five. What the hell. I put it into his hand.

"Been disoriented since '36," the street guy said. "How long is that?"

"Six years," I said.

The guy shook his head and reached down for a frayed blue shoulder bag.

"I'm straight on the time of day," he said, his hands still trembling. "But damned if I can get the years straight. You gave me a bill?"

"A five," I said.

"You don't look so good yourself," he said, trying to focus on me.

Somewhere down the alley some kids laughed, not at us but at some joke behind a fence.

"Deacon Ortiz tried to kill me," I said.

"Never trust the church," he said, sitting on the curb and looking at the five-dollar bill.

"Sure you're okay?" I asked.

"I'm alive," the guy said. "And I've got five bucks. Sometimes when you don't expect it, life is good for a few hours."

"Amen," I said.

"Wait," he said as I turned to walk toward Lorna's address. "I know you."

"I don't think so," I said.

"Your name's Peters," he said. "Before I lost touch, I worked at Santiago's gas station in Encino."

"Farkas?" I asked. "I was thinking about you the other day."

"Small world," he said, looking up at the sky. "Few minutes ago I see Samson and now you. Remember Santiago?"

I remembered him but I didn't want to think about it now. I'd picked up a few dollars riding shotgun at Santiago's Shell Station in Encino. Things were relatively quiet on the ten-to-midnight shift one night. A fat couple walking down the street pushing a grocery cart they'd stolen from Ralph's started to fight about who-knows-what. I watched them as I sat sipping Pepsi on a rickety lawn chair in front of Santiago's station, listening to "Amos 'n' Andy" on the radio while a wiry ex-con named Snick Farkas pumped gas. Farkas was the guy who loved classical music. Said he'd memorized twenty operas in prison. Volunteered to sing them to anyone who would listen. No one would listen.

Santiago, who was over seventy and had a bad leg, had once taken a few shots at a kid who had pulled the gas-stealing trick twice. The shots had taken out windows in the stores across the street and almost hit an alderman named Blankenship, who was walking down the street with a woman he later claimed was his cousin but who everyone knew was a prostitute from San Diego. Santiago decided to call it quits, but his brother, a junior partner in the station, had talked him into trying again. Santiago had grumbled but decided to make the final try.

But things got worse. There was an increase in hold-ups of the station by frustrated kids, pre-Zoot-suiters who counted on free gas from Santiago. There had been four hold-ups in one month, all on the night shift when Santiago wasn't there. That was when I had been hired.

The first week I was on the job Santiago insisted on hiding inside the station with his shotgun. He looked like a grizzled Mexican Gabby Hayes, right down to the game leg. His greasy Shell baseball cap cut into the illusion but didn't kill it. Farkas pumped gas, his hooded eyes revealing nothing. I sat in the lawn chair, wearing my .38 and a gray sweatshirt over my not-so-good jeans.

About eleven that night a car full of kids pulled into the station in a 1933 Chevy. Two boys no older than fifteen got out of the car. A girl in the back seat was laughing and holding her sides. One of the boys, who was holding a sawed-off rifle, told her to shut up.

Farkas stood calmly, wiping oil from his hands. Later he told me that he was one-quarter Apache and his grandfather had taught him that he was part of the Great Oneness and would join it one day. Farkas had led a wild life before the truth of his grandfather's words hit him, but once they did, he began to prepare himself for the Great Oneness. The night those two boys came out of the car seemed, to Farkas, a decent enough night to die.

Before either boy could say anything, Santiago, standing inside the station, blew out his own front window with a blast that rained glass on me, Farkas, the Chevy, and the robbers.

"Loco shit!" the kid with the rifle had said, ducking behind the car.

The other kid—skinny, with the eyes of someone who loved the Lady of White Powder—blinked. His cheek was bleeding from flying glass. The butt of a pistol showed from his pocket, but he didn't reach for it.

My .38 was out before the shards had stopped raining on the gas pumps. The girl in the car wasn't laughing anymore. The kid behind the car with the shotgun was cursing. The skinny kid in front of the car stood stunned and looked at Farkas. I looked at Farkas, too, as I held my gun on the kid. Farkas smiled a smile that said "Give it up" and I could see that the kid was giving it up, but Santiago came hobbling through his broken window. The kid with the shotgun stood up, aimed at no one in particular, and fired. The shot took out pump number two. Santiago was gurgling with joy as he fired in return, taking out the front window of the Chevy.

The kid with the shotgun jumped into the car, and I nodded at the skinny kid to climb in with him. As he reached for the rear door, the girl inside screamed and the car burned rubber and took off. The skinny kid stood wide-eyed in the driveway of Santiago's station and watched his partner drive off. Santiago chortled with pleasure and aimed at the kid.

"Go for your gun, *ladron*," Santiago challenged.

The dazed skinny kid looked at the mad old man in the Shell baseball cap and started to reach for the gun in his pocket.

"Hold it," I shouted and the kid stopped.

Santiago cursed.

"I want to kill somebody," the old man hissed. "I am unfulfilled."

"Go home and play with yourself," I said. To the kid I said, "Take off."

The skinny kid scuttled off in the same direction his friend had driven.

I remembered that night, all right. I had made the mistake of telling Anne about it. I'd come home on top of the world and twenty bucks richer, ready to buy her flowers and a damn-the-Depression dinner at Chasen's. I told her the story and she packed and said it was the end.

"I remember, Farkas," I said. "Thanks for the memory. If the cops show up and you're still sitting here, send them up to apartment six-D. Got it?"

"Got it," he said, holding up the five. "They're doin' an opera somewhere near here sometime soon. Maybe I can find it and buy a ticket. Today's my lucky day. Come back any time and run me over. We'll talk about old times."

"Old times," I said, thinking of Anne.

I looked up at Lorna Bartholomew's building. It was a six-story, trying to bring up the neighborhood and failing.

I stepped into the lobby foyer. An old man in a ratty gray sweater and a little badge sat on a bridge chair reading the latest issue of *Atlantic Monthly*. He didn't look up.

"Pardon me," I said.

He looked up.

"Bob La Follette's worrying about prohibition making a

comeback," he said, pointing to the article on his lap. "Can you imagine with what's going on in the world someone worrying about people drinking?"

"No," I said. "I'd like to see Miss Bartholomew."

"Name?" he asked.

"Peters."

The old man nodded. I looked out into the street. No cops yet. Farkas was sitting there admiring the five I had given him and remembering the good old days in Los Angeles.

"First name?"

"Toby."

"Check," he said, and picked up the house phone. "Peters here."

He hung up, reached under the wooden counter, and the inner lobby door clicked open.

"Six-D," he said. "She said you can come on up." The old man sank back in his seat with his magazine.

The lobby was full of glass and mirror, with a cracked white tile floor. No people. The inner lobby door clicked closed behind me, and I headed for the elevator. It was waiting and open. I got in and pushed six, thinking the place was a lot like the one Anne had moved into after walking out on me.

When the elevator opened, I thought I heard a door close, but no one was in the hallway. Six-D was halfway down the corridor to my left. All the doors I passed were the same except for 6-D, which was open. I hoped Lorna had simply opened it when the old doorman called, but she wasn't standing just inside waiting for me. I expected Miguelito to come yapping out of the shadows and go for my throat, but there was nothing.

"Lorna?" I called, stepping into darkness.

My foot hit something that went skittering across the floor. I pulled out my .38 and got out of the light from the door. "Lorna?" I called out again, more softly.

There was no answer. I reached for a light switch on the wall against which I was leaning, found none, and moved back to the open apartment door, there I found a switch, hit it, and turned, gun leveled into the room.

I saw that in the darkness I had kicked a lamp. The lamp didn't belong on the floor. Neither did most of what was on the floor in the alcove and in the living room beyond. The place was a mess. A mad baboon had been let loose, or the Stanford football team had had a party. The sofa was turned over and ripped open. The radio was smashed and on its back on the floor. Two matching stuffed chairs no longer matched and probably wouldn't be worth fixing. Even the carpeting had been torn up, but nothing had been torn up as much as Lorna, who lay sprawled on the floor.

"Lorna," I whispered, and I thought she moved, but I didn't go to her. Someone had answered the doorman's call and it hadn't been her. Whoever it was might still be here. I moved to the windows and threw open the drapes, letting in sunlight.

Then I kicked open the bathroom door. This room had been attacked, too. Medicine cabinet open, broken bottles on the floor. And the bedroom had been chewed up by a giant lawn mower while the kitchen was a swamp of food, drink, and ice cubes on the floor. The refrigerator door was open and everything, even the box of Arm and Hammer, had been pulled out and thrown to the floor or in the general direction of the sink. A dog-food dish was upside down in a corner.

Sure now that no one was there but me, I closed the front door and hurried to Lorna. I kneeled next to her and touched her face. It was cool and turning white.

"Lorna?" I asked, but the question was really *Are you alive?* Lorna's eyelids fluttered open. She looked to her left like a disoriented newborn baby and then up at me. A trickle of blood meandered from the corner of her red mouth down her chin.

Her mouth moved, forming a word but no sound.

"He?" I asked.

Her eyes fluttered, and she looked like she was going back into her sleep.

"I've gotta call an ambulance."

She grasped my hand, her fingernails cutting into the flesh of my palms. She had more to say.

"We," she gasped.

"We?" I asked.

The eyes fluttered. "We are the Phantom."

"Who did this?" I asked, my face near enough hers to taste her bloody breath.

"Lorna's mouth opened. "Rance and Johnson. And Minnie. Don't forget Minnie."

"Minnie?" I asked.

"Miguelito," she answered.

"Miguelito did this?"

She shook her head. "Ask Miguelito," she gasped, and made a motion with her right hand. "Shave," she whispered.

I touched my cheek. I needed a shave all right, but this wasn't the time to talk about it. She convulsed in my arms, reached up, trying to grab for life, and scratched her fingers across my face. Then she was dead.

Reactions came quickly. The first was a weariness, the most overwhelming sense of being tired that I had ever felt. I wanted to turn over the ripped sofa and take a nap.

Think, I told myself. Think. I got up, staggered to the door to the small balcony. It was open. I could see the bay. The apartment was right at the edge of the water. I stepped out and caught the bay breeze and smell of fish.

Someone had killed Lorna and wanted something she had, had torn the apartment apart to find it. Either he had gone through everything and found whatever it was he was looking for in the last place he looked, or it was still somewhere and I might find it, whatever it was.

I didn't find the knife that had been used on Lorna. I figured the killer—or killers, if Lorna was right—had taken it away. Or had pitched it out the window into the ocean. I imagined the bloody knife spinning on the way down, catching the reflection of the sun, clanking against the rocks and flipping into the water.

I touched my forehead to see if I was feverish and my hand came back red with blood. My cheek was bleeding where Lorna had reached for me in her last shudder.

I went into the kitchen, found an unbroken glass on the counter near the sink, and got a drink of cool water from the tap. Then I used a clean dish towel to wipe the blood from my cheek. There was something I should be doing, but I wasn't sure what it was. I leaned forward over the kitchen sink. Somewhere beyond the window I heard a siren.

Then my brain kicked into second gear. Lorna Bartholomew was dead. My face was scratched. The murder weapon was missing. With a little help from a classy assistant district attorney and the testimony of a doorman, I would make a pretty good murder suspect.

Lorna hadn't answered the house phone. The killer had probably just given a high-pitched grunt. The killer knew someone was coming up. The killer, in fact, knew that someone named Peters was coming up. I had been announced.

It was time to move. I went from the kitchen into the bedroom, avoiding the living room where Lorna's body lay. I found the phone, but it had been ripped from the wall.

I was standing there with the dead phone in my hand when the door to the apartment pushed open and a uniformed cop came in with a service revolver in his hand.

"Don't move," he croaked.

He was young enough to be my son. I didn't move.

He looked around quickly. Sweat was building on his forehead.

"What's going on?"

"Woman's murdered," I answered. "In the other room."

"Against the wall," the cop ordered.

I moved to the wall, spread my legs, and leaned forward.

The cop came behind me, reached under my arm, and removed my .38 from my pocket.

"Where's the phone?"

"Busted," I said, turning part way to show it to him.

"Great," the cop said.

"Use the intercom," I suggested. "Doorman can call for backup."

"Thanks," he said, and called the doorman.

"I had someone call a Sergeant Preston and an Inspector Sunset," I said.

"Head down," the cop said, and told the doorman to call in a murder in apartment 6-D.

The young cop cuffed me, had me sit down on a kitchen chair that hadn't been busted up, and we waited after he checked Lorna to be sure she was dead. It was more than he wanted to handle. I tried to talk to him but he told me to be quiet. He did what a lot of scared cops do, overcompensated. Basic psych book stuff. He told me to shut up. I shut up. If I didn't, the psych books say he might have started in on me.

Less than five minutes later Preston and Sunset came through the door.

"What've we got . . . ?"

"Brummel. Got a homicide. In there. Found the suspect on the scene."

"You guys didn't exactly fly here," I said.

Preston glanced at me.

"Peters," Preston said, as Sunset knelt to examine Lorna's body, "I've had a long, bad night, and you're going to make the day worse and longer. I've got a headache and I'm hungry, so if you just want to confess and get this over with . . ."

"I didn't kill her," I said.

"Suit yourself," Preston said with a deep sigh, looking at the scratches on my bloody cheek.

"Preston," I said. "I had you called. Would I call you and tell you to come if I planned to kill her?"

"Remember Barnes," Sunset said from Lorna's body.

"Gus Barnes," Preston explained to me. "Few months back. Called. Said someone just called and said he was on the way over to kill his wife. Told the desk man to hurry. We got a car there in six minutes."

"Five-eleven, Sarge," said Sunset, standing up. "She's dead."

"Barnes killed his wife," said Preston, nodding and rubbing the bridge of his nose. "Messed it up. Your having us called doesn't prove diddle-daddle."

"Diddle-daddle?"

"Sorry," he said. "Hard to be creative on an hour of sleep."

"Why would I kill her?"

"Hired," said Sunset.

"Spurned," added Preston.

"Accident," said Sunset.

"Wouldn't pay blackmail," said Preston.

"Enough," I said. "Let me make a call."

"You see a phone?" asked Preston. "I mean one you didn't tear off the wall?"

"I didn't do it, Preston," I said.

Brummel, the first cop, came back. About twelve minutes after that a bunch of cops came in, and I was escorted from the apartment by Preston, who said his wife would make him sleep in the guest room tonight if he ever got home. I told him I felt sorry for him. He thanked me.

10

The Bayfront Police Station wasn't on the bay and barely deserved the title "station." The core of the station was an old red stone building that looked as if it had once been a firehouse. It had been added to over at least three generations, each generation contributing a different color of stone. The wing to the left of the entrance was gray brick, and the right wing a combination of reds, yellows, grays, and even almost-blacks.

A sergeant named Cunningham with red hair, suspenders, and very bad teeth took my wallet, comb, and the lint from my pockets less than a minute after we went in. A half-asleep Amazon woman in a blue uniform took my picture, and then Preston and Sunset led me up a flight of stairs to a small interrogation room with yellow walls that reminded me of my brother's office in the Wilshire Station back in Los Angeles. Preston and Sunset spoke to me sincerely for about twenty minutes, letting me know I was in very deep diddle-daddle.

"Peters," Preston leaned over and whispered, "you are

108

nailed. You wanna give us some details so we can all get a night's sleep?"

"I didn't kill her," I said. "I was there to protect her from someone. Stokowski hired me to protect, not murder, remember?"

"You did good work," sighed Sunset, looking around for something to use as an imaginary bat.

"Who?" asked Preston, wearily drinking something hot from a paper cup. "Who were you protecting her from? Oh, yeah. The Phantom of the Opera."

"Maybe," said Sunset brightly, sizing up a rolled San Francisco *Chronicle* for use as an imaginary Louisville Slugger, "he killed her for the publicity. Phantom strikes. Fill the seats."

"Forgive him," Preston said to me quietly.

"He's forgiven," I said. "What about me?"

"Not so easy," sighed Preston. "You didn't do it, who did? Doorman says she told you to come up. Few minutes later we find you with the body, scratches on your face, phone in your hand ripped from the wall."

"She said a couple of guys named Rance and Johnson and a woman named Minnie did it."

"Minnie?" Preston groaned, kneading the bridge of his nose.

"She also said I should ask Miguelito," I added.

"Miguelito?"

"Her dog."

Sunset, who had moved behind me, hit me with the rolled-up newspaper. My head jerked forward.

"Sorry," Sunset said. "Big fly on your head."

"Cut that shit," Preston ordered, stepping behind me so I had to turn my head to watch the two cops. Preston was smaller, but older and presumably wiser. Sunset shrugged and came back in front of the table to hit a few imaginary balls through the grimy wall.

"Thanks," I said over my shoulder to Preston.

He ran a hand through his graying hair and threw his empty coffee cup in the general direction of the overfull wastebasket in the corner. The wastebasket had one of those paper liners two sizes too big for the basket.

"And I want a phone call," I said.

"Who's stopping you?" asked Preston, pointing to the phone on the table. "Hey, make two, three calls. No long distance."

"All you had to do was ask," said Sunset.

I picked up the phone and called information. I got Lundeen's number. The phone rang six times before Lundeen answered.

"It's me, Toby Peters," I said. "Are you sitting?"

"Whenever I can," he said with a deep sigh.

And I told him. I'll give him credit. He didn't say much. He did groan from time to time, and his voice wasn't steady, but he said he'd have a lawyer there as quickly as he could.

"Peters," he said with a tear in his voice, "I must say this. I never really liked Lorna. I didn't know her well, but I didn't like her and now . . . You didn't kill her?"

"John," I said, "why the hell would I kill her?"

"I'm sorry," he said. "I . . . Lord, 'O happy dagger. This is thy sheath; there rust, and let me die.' "

"Beautiful, John," I said. The two cops looked at me with weariness in their drooping eyes.

"Gounod," he said. "*Roméo et Juliette.* Actually, the words are Shakespeare's, but . . ."

"John, find Gunther, Jeremy, and Shelly," I said. "Tell them not to come here, to stay on the job. Got it?"

"I have it," he said.

"And send a lawyer, fast," I said. "You have Vera's number?"

He had it. Or rather he knew the hotel she was staying at and looked up the number while I waited. When he hung up I called. The phone rang six times and then a man answered. It was Martin Passacaglia. I heard a dog yapping behind him. I hung up.

I passed the time waiting for the lawyer feeling sorry for myself. Preston and Sunset played scare-the-suspect.

"Open . . ." Preston began.

". . . and shut," Sunset agreed. "Witnesses say he entered about ten. We get a call that a murder is in progress seconds later, dispatch a car, and catch him with a mess—scratches on his face, and a very newly dead body. Open . . ."

". . . and shut," Preston finished.

I didn't say anything.

Preston sang a medley of Russ Columbo, Harry Cool, and Bing Crosby songs.

"What do you think? Could have been a crooner?" he asked.

"Lovely voice," I said. "None of the new guys have the timbre. Maybe Buddy Clark, Perry Como."

When Preston started "Just One More Chance" for the third time at about two-thirty in the morning, Sunset left, announcing that he "had to take a leak." Preston took the news solemnly and sat across from me, waiting with his arms folded.

"You like baseball?" I asked.

"I like singing and I like quiet," Preston said. "I like being home with my wife and kids when my shift is over. I don't like catching murder calls, and I don't like talking baseball with out-of-town private dicks."

I shrugged and shut up. He sat quietly, arms folded, out of songs.

The lawyer arrived at a little after three, escorted in by Sunset, who smiled at Preston and me. I didn't like the smile. The lawyer was a little Mexican guy about sixty-five. His back was straight, his face clean-shaven except for a mustache, his three-piece beige suit recently pressed, his tan shoes highly polished. He nodded at me and the two cops and placed his briefcase on the table.

"Gentlemen," he said.

"Counselor," said Preston, sitting on the edge of the table and looking at his watch. "You want some time alone with your client?"

"Absolutely," he answered.

Preston and Sunset moved toward the door, but the little lawyer held up his hand.

"Not in this room," he said. "I want privacy. You wouldn't want your case thrown out later because you failed to honor the lawyer-client relationship?"

In short, the lawyer was telling them the room had a hidden mike and he knew it. Now we all knew it.

"Bathroom's down the hall to the right," Preston said. "Inspector Sunset will show you."

The lawyer picked up his briefcase, adjusted his jacket and vest, and we followed Sunset into the hall. Sunset led us to the washroom and made it clear he would be waiting outside the door for us. There were two windows in the room, both open a crack to let some of the smell of Lysol out and some of the smell of the night air in. Four urinals, their white showing rust patterns, stood along one wall alongside two stalls without doors. Opposite urinals and stalls were two sinks.

The lawyer, who identified himself as Manuel Flores, turned on the water in all four faucets and talked softly, our heads close enough together that I could smell his aftershave. I told him everything. It took about five minutes. Then he asked questions. That took about fifteen minutes.

"*Basta*," he said when he had finished. "We have a problem. All they have is circumstantial evidence, but that is all they need. The law says they must establish your guilt beyond a reasonable doubt. That means there can be some doubt as long as the jury, if there is a jury, is convinced that you have committed the crime. But what is a *reasonable* doubt?"

"You really think they're going to hold me for this?" I asked.

Lawyer Flores shook his head to show he wasn't sure. He washed his hands, patted down his hair, checked his mustache in the spotted mirror, and led me to the door where Sunset was standing guard.

Back in the little interrogation room, Flores pulled up a chair and sat at the table with me at his side. "I would like to hear charges and cause before deciding my client's course of action," he said, opening his briefcase. He took out a fresh white pad, removed his Waterman pen from his jacket pocket, and looked at Preston. Sunset stood in the corner, arms folded.

"Your client's fingerprints," Preston added, after he had gone over what else he had on me, "are all over the apartment. Just got a call from forensics. He was in that apartment with a dead woman looking for something, probably money, when a patrolman arrived. Also, we have testimony that your client had a fight with the deceased this morning."

"Fight?" I said. "You . . ."

"Weapon?" Lawyer Flores interrupted, taking notes.

"Missing," said Sunset. "There's a balcony and the bay right outside the window. It'd take a good throw, but our Peters here looks like he's got a whippy little arm. We'll look in the morning, but it could have been washed clear down to San Jose by now."

"Why do you not believe the Bartholomew woman was dead when my client went up to her apartment?" Flores asked.

"Doorman called up when he arrived," said Preston wearily. "Miss Bartholomew told him to send said client up."

"How does the doorman know it was the Bartholomew woman who answered?" Flores asked. "An intercom phone, a word, a uh-huh in answer to the doorman's question if he should send my client up. Why could it not be the killer who answered the call?"

Preston shrugged and Sunset sighed. They had heard this kind of thing before.

"What are you fishing for, Señor Lawyer?" Sunset asked.

"My client answers questions," Lawyer Flores said. "In return for the state's attorney setting reasonable bond."

"State's attorney says we go for murder one," said Preston. "Just talked to him. Asking for a hold without bond."

"I need a toilet," I said, standing up.

"You were just in the toilet," said Sunset. "Something wrong with your fucking guts? Your lawyer slip you some greasy tacos or something?"

Lawyer Flores was looking at his legal pad notes, tapping his pen point in the margin. He looked up at Sunset, who tried to hold Flores' gaze, but Sunset was a kitten and Lawyer Flores a tiger.

"I will be filing a grievance with the community relations section of the police department," Flores said. "The grievance will cite your ethnic insults. This is not a threat, Sergeant. It is a piece of information so that you can prepare for the inquiry."

"Confession," suggested Preston. "And maybe we can recommend aggravated manslaughter. Maybe your client was high on reefers. Hell, maybe the lady threatened him and he had to take her knife away. Self-defense. Be creative."

"I'm about to piss in my pants," I said.

"Take him," sighed Preston.

Sunset pushed away from the wall, made a sour face, and pointed to the door. Lawyer Flores was trying to be creative, but he didn't have many blocks to play with.

"Taco lawyer isn't going to do you shit, Peters," Sunset informed me as we headed back down the dim hallway to the men's room. "You got a long wait in County and then a long vacation in Folsom."

I started into the washroom with Sunset no more than a step behind. I had no doubt that if I dropped my drawers and sat on the toilet he would stand and watch and criticize my technique. But I wasn't going to give him that chance. I grabbed the end of the door, stepped to my left, and jerked the door back as hard as I could into Sunset as he took a step into the room.

He didn't fall, but he did let out a woomph sound and slid down the slimy wall, his hand going automatically for the pistol in his holster. I got it first and gave him a little push with my foot that sent him the rest of the way to the floor. His head hit the tile and bounced like a baseball on concrete. I backed up toward the windows, pointing his gun at him.

Sunset was stunned but he wasn't out. He tried to sit up and slipped. I went for the first window—put my free hand under the opening and pushed up. It didn't budge. I looked back at Sunset, who was sitting up now. I tried the second window. It wouldn't budge either.

"Don't panic," I told myself. "Calm. Be calm."

I shook my arms in warmup, took a deep breath of stench, and used the back end of Sunset's pistol to break the window. It made a hell of a lot of noise as the glass fell and cracked in the alley one floor below.

Sunset made an uncoordinated lunge for me from the floor. I got out of the way, pushed a few standing shards of glass away, and looked out the window as he got to his knees, shaking his head to clear it.

The alley was one floor down.

"I'll tear your . . ." Sunset growled as I started to climb out the window. He put his hand on the nearby sink to try to pull himself up.

"I'm going to do you a favor, Sunset," I said, looking back. "Little friendly secret between you and me."

I flipped open the pistol, dropped the bullets into the sink, where they skittered toward the drain, flipped the pistol closed, and threw the empty weapon across the room.

"Go get your gun, Inspector," I went on, easing myself out the window as Sunset made it to his feet. "No one has to know I took it from you. Just tell them I went out the window as soon as we got through the door. Our secret, gringo."

I jumped. I didn't want to jump. I was afraid to jump. But it was better than being locked up and having the key shipped to Peru. I jumped in the general direction of a pile of garbage stacked next to rusty trash cans. I hit the garbage feet first. I landed on an oversized paper bag that popped open like a balloon, and I went rolling in the oily alley. Above me I could hear Sunset scrambling for his gun and bullets. I got to my feet and lurched to the entrance of the alley. I was too old for this kind of thing. I was too old for most kinds of things, but I wasn't going to admit it, not even to myself. Behind and above me, Sunset was not calling for my surrender.

"Halt," he yelled. "Or I'll fire."

"I'm not armed," I said.

"Who gives a shit?" he bellowed, and took a shot at me.

I went around the corner to the street as two more shots tore up brickwork. The street was empty. The sun was setting behind a row of apartment buildings across the street. I hurried across that street and tried to leap the small metal fence of the first building. I settled for scrambling over. I moved to the side of the apartment building and ducked into a concrete-paved walk to the back of the building. From the darkness I looked back across the street at the station entrance. A spurt of four cops came out, all with guns in their hands. Sunset and Preston were two of the cops. They started to fan out. Preston went left, mumbling to himself. Sunset went right into the sunset. Cop Three crossed the street, and Cop Four looked as if he were heading straight at me.

I turned, moved slowly around the building in the darkness till I hit the backyard and the lawn. The back fence was a little higher than the front. I ran across the lawn and went over that fence as if I were in spring training in Arizona, and then I was on my way.

I had a dog to find and I knew where to look.

11

I found a Plymouth with the back door open about four blocks from the police station. I got in, locked the door, and curled up on the floor. Maybe the search would pass me by. I needed some sleep. I needed something to eat. I needed to think.

My car was probably still parked in front of Lorna's apartment building if the cops hadn't taken it in. I could have found a cab or hopped a bus if I had money, but I didn't have money. The cops had my money, my wallet, my pencil, my notebook, my old man's watch, and my keys in a paper bag. I curled up and closed my eyes. I can't say I slept. I discovered one thing. A man with a bad back shouldn't spend the night on the floor of a Plymouth.

When I thought the first light of dawn was promising to hit the street, I crawled out of the car and looked around. The street was empty.

I slouched into an alley heading south, looking up at the sky every few seconds to watch for the first sure signs of dawn. I must have been tired but I didn't feel it. I must have been tired, because I didn't hear the patrol car turn into the alley behind me. I was moving along close to the fences and garages on the right. The beam of the car's headlights bounced in front of me, catching an early morning cat who stared, eyes glowing for a second, and then ran off. I ducked into a yard and crouched down behind a bush.

The patrol car came slowly, so I knew they hadn't seen me. A small spotlight scanned yards and garbage cans.

The cops in the car didn't have the heart for hard looking. They were probably at the end of a shift and tired or just starting a shift and not yet fully awake. I knew the feeling. I'd gone through it as a beat cop back in Glendale. The car bounced slowly past me, pausing for an instant to scan the yard and bushes. The beam caught my face momentarily. I closed my eyes and they passed on. I stayed crouching while the car rumbled past, and then I got up. I was about to continue on my way when the headlights of the cop car sent twin white probes down the alley again. They had turned around and were moving slowly back. I was next to a garage. I tried the door. It was locked, but it was a lock that should have been ashamed of itself. In the gray light of dawn, I found a rusty nail. Now I could hear voices from the returning cop car. I used the nail to open the garage door and threw the nail away.

There were two windows in the garage, both covered with curtains. I closed the garage door behind me and made my way to one of the windows, following the gray light that seeped through the dirty curtains. I banged my ankle against something hard and felt the skin break under my pants. The patrol car had stopped just outside the garage. I could hear the engine. I could hear the voices as the cops got out.

"Right there, by those bushes," came a voice.

"So why didn't you say so when we came past?" came a rasping complaint.

"I . . . I just wasn't sure, and you were talking," the first voice said.

A flashlight beam scanned the curtains of the garage and footsteps moved across the grass.

"Well," sighed the raspy cop.

I held my breath and waited. And then they stopped, and one of them started to try the door

"Maybe I just . . ." he began.

"Maybe you just," the raspy voice agreed. "Let's get over to Mel's and have something to eat."

The car doors closed and the engine hummed away, but I didn't move for a few seconds. I pushed back the curtain and found myself looking into the eyes of an alley cat who was perched on the ledge outside. San Francisco was filled with cats. I'd have to tell Dash about this.

Then I turned around. This was not the simple one-car garage of a happy family with a mom and pop and a couple of fat kids. The place was full of bicycles and parts of bicycles. Tires and wheels hung from hooks on the ceiling. Biking helmets and handlebars were mounted on one wall like a hunter's antler trophies. A table in one corner was lined with cans of paint. Either Santa Claus lived here or I'd stumbled on a stolen bicycle shop.

My heart soared like a bird. I could be a self-righteous thief. I could steal a bike and feel like MacArthur liberating stolen property and giving it to a deserving peasant, me. I picked the nearest bike, a man's bike with a bad paint job. I didn't have time to go quietly through the pile. It would have to do. I found a dirty white painter's cap with the word ZOSH printed across the brow in nail polish or something else red, and plunked it on my head.

I wheeled the bike to the door, opened the door, and went outside. Dawn was coming fast. I could see light from the sun. I looked into the alley. No cop car. I looked back at the house behind the garage and something caught my eye. A man was standing in the second-floor window looking out at me. He was big, bearded, and naked, and he did not like what he saw.

He threw open the window as I ran the bike into the alley and jumped on.

"You goddamn thief," the man hissed, but he didn't yell, which confirmed my belief that this bike and the others weren't kosher. The man wasn't shouting for help or running after me with a gun. The man was a thief, and he was taking his losses rather than draw attention to himself and his vocation.

I was pumping like crazy just in case the man in the window decided not to take his loss easily. I sailed into the street and felt a gentle push of wind off the ocean. It was a cool morning, but I took off my shirt as I rode and stuffed it under the handlebars. An overaged morning biker, head down, racing against a stopwatch in his mind.

I decided to stick to side streets. People were getting up and out of their houses and apartments. Kids were slouching bleary-eyed out to the curb to catch school buses. A truck inched past me and the guy inside hurled a bundle of San Francisco *Chronicles* past my head onto the front steps of a brownstone house.

I don't know what time I hit downtown. I had no watch. I biked straight up the street, head down, pumping as hard as I could, not looking right or left. I asked an old black woman with a shopping bag how to get to the Trocadero Hotel. I found it at the bottom of a hill right next to a cable car turnaround. A couple of men and a woman were pushing a cable car to point it back up the hill.

I parked the bike against a tree. There was a good chance the bike would be stolen, but the bike was accustomed to that by now. I shoved the Zosh hat in my back pocket and put my shirt back on. It was a wrinkled mess. I looked at myself in the window of a drugstore. I was a mess of wild hair, sticking straight up from wearing the cap, and bristly gray hair on my face from not shaving. What the hell. I walked into the lobby of the Trocadero Hotel as the cable car clanged behind me to let people know it was ready to roll.

The hotel was small, the lobby narrow. A skinny old man in a dark suit was standing behind the counter drinking a cup of coffee and going through a stack of cards. He looked up at me and stopped.

"Miss Tenatti's room," I said.

He didn't move.

"It's been a tough night," I said, reaching over to shake his hand. "I can see you recognize me. We've been shooting down by the wharf."

"I . . ." the old man began.

"Buster Crabbe," I said, showing my profile. "Haven't had time to get out of costume."

"I don't . . ." the old man said, looking around for help.

"Just give Vera a call and tell her Toby is here," I said, leaning over confidentially. "That's our private name. You understand."

"Private . . . yes, Mr. Crabbe," he said, and picked up the phone, keeping his eyes on me.

I grinned and looked around as if I were considering buying the place.

"Miss Tenatti? Yes. Mr. Buster Crabbe is . . ."

"Tell her Toby," I interrupted.

"Toby," he corrected. "Yes. Of course."

He hung up and looked at me.

"She said you should come right up," he said. "Room four-fourteen. You look much different in your films."

"Makeup," I said, taking a step toward the elevator.

"Now or in the movies?" he asked.

I laughed falsely and stepped into the elevator. The elevator woman glanced at the desk clerk, who nodded that it was all right to take me up.

Vera was waiting for me at the open door. She was wearing a silky pink nightgown.

"You look terrible," she said, putting her hand to her mouth and stepping back to let me in.

I went into the room, looked around for Passacaglia, and plopped on the unmade bed. From nowhere Miguelito leaped onto my chest and tried to eat one of my shirt buttons. I petted him. He didn't bite.

"The police are looking for you," Vera said.

"I know," I said, my eyes closed. "You have anything to eat?"

"No . . . yes, some doughnuts," she said. "But I'm starting on health food to . . . Lorna's dead."

I pushed Miguelito away and sat up as Vera handed me a dish with two doughnuts.

"She's dead," I agreed.

"They think you killed her," Vera said, touching her bee-stung lower lip with her thumb. Her pink silk gown opened slightly at her breasts.

I downed the doughnuts.

"Anything to drink?" I asked.

"Water?"

I got out of bed and moved into the small bathroom. I filled a glass and drank five glasses of not-quite-cool water. Vera and the dog watched me. I looked at her in the mirror. She looked soft and fresh. I looked at myself. I looked like a hairy, overripe avocado.

"You have a razor?"

"Yes, in the cabinet. Fresh blades are . . . you'll see them."

I took off my shirt, opened the cabinet, found the razor, put in a blade, and shaved as we talked.

"Who would kill Lorna?" she asked.

"Rance, Johnson, and Minnie," I said. "She told me before she died. You know them?"

"Rance, John . . . They're characters in *La Fanciulla del West*," she said.

"Interesting. She also told me to shave," I said. "I'm shaving."

I finished, found some toothpowder, rubbed it on my

teeth, washed my face, and ran my fingers through my hair. I looked in the mirror and saw something that resembled a tired me.

"I'm supposed to go to a rehearsal," she said. "At ten. With Lorna dead . . . I don't . . . I don't belong here. Martin came here last night. He tried to . . . I shouldn't be here. And what am I going to do with Miguelito?"

I turned to Vera. She came into my arms, her pink night-gown coming open.

"I'll find him a home," I said.

"Thank you. You need a little rest and I need a little comforting," she said, starting to cry. "Would you lie down with me for just a few minutes?"

I was tired and she was far from home and she reminded me of Anne and I don't know who I reminded her of but that's why it happened. It was fast, sweet, soft, and interrupted by Miguelito, who didn't know what was going on and probably wondered when Lorna was coming to get him.

I slept and dreamed of Snick Farkas sitting in Santiago's gas station dressed in a cape and wearing a white mask. Farkas was trying to sing something to me. He was saying a name, but I couldn't make it out, and then as I slept I remembered: He said he had seen Samson going into Lorna's building.

When I woke up, Vera was gone and Miguelito was lying on the bed looking up at me. His ears rose when my eyes opened. I found a note from Vera saying she had to go to the final dress rehearsal, that I was welcome to stay in the room and wait for her, that I should take care of Miguelito.

It was a nice offer, and I considered room service when I couldn't find any cash, but I had a killer to find and my neck to save. I put my shirt back on, found a leash for Miguelito, and came up with a plan.

The desk clerk pretended to ignore me when I stepped out of the elevator, but even cleaned up and shaved I didn't look much like Buster Crabbe. I gave him a smile and moved Miguelito's paw in a wave. The clerk pretended not to see.

The bike was where I had left it, though a seedy-looking wino was circling it slowly. Lorna had either been delirious, making sense, or both. It wasn't me she wanted to shave. It was Miguelito.

12

I tied Miguelito's leash to the handlebars, put on my Zosh hat, and started to pedal down the street slowly so the dog could keep up. He was well fed and having a good time. We were pals. The streets were alive now and the morning was showing signs of getting hot. I turned a corner, moving away from downtown.

Three kids were throwing a football around on the street. An old man with no teeth and wearing a hat with a wide brim used his cane to make his baggy-pantsed way down the sidewalk, and a fat woman with a pretty face leaned out of a second-story window to call down to a thin man who looked up at her, sweat forming under the arms of his tan suit.

I put my head down and pedaled. I went slowly so Miguelito could keep up, but he wasn't used to this sort of thing. After two blocks he stopped suddenly. Just stopped and sat down. I had a choice of holding on to the leash and taking a fall or letting him go and risk having to chase him around the neighborhood.

I let go of the leash. Miguelito didn't run. He sat panting on the curb. I coaxed, pleaded, threatened, but Miguelito had had enough. He wouldn't even look me in the eye. The old man with the hat and cane caught up to us, looked at the dog, and said, "Shoot him."

He held up his crippled hand to form a pistol with his fingers and feigned shooting the dog, but Miguelito ignored him.

"Thanks," I said.

"Between the eyes," the old man said, pointing his finger gun between his own eyes. "Dog that don't do as he is told should be shot as an example to others."

"What others?" I asked.

"Shoot him," the old man repeated.

"I'll think about it," I said.

"Think about it," the old man said with contempt. "We'd be up to our gazoonkis in Nazis and Japs if Patton and MacArthur sat around thinking instead of shooting. Think about it."

The old man gave up and headed for a bar on the corner.

Miguelito had stopped in front of a pawn shop. RUDOLFO CASTILLO'S TROPIC PAWN SHOP, the sign said. The shop was steel-gated but an old man had stopped in front of the gate and was pulling out a key. I picked up the dog, held him propped against the handlebars, and wheeled toward the shop.

The man, who I figured was probably Castillo, looked as old as the mountains of hell. He was a brown, wrinkled man, wearing a wrinkled herringbone suit with no tie. The suit was about two sizes too big for him. He opened the padlock on the steel gates that protected the door to his shop and looked at me and the dog as if this were the start of another bad day. I waited till he pushed the gates open and then followed him inside. The place brought back a childhood memory, triggered more by the smell than by the familiar line-up of guitars, portable radios, watches, rings, necklaces, harmonicas, trumpets, and weapons. The smell made a special tug at my memory.

I grunted in with the dog in my arms.

"Rudolfo Castillo at your service and open for business," said the little old man as he moved slowly behind his counter, pulled open the little window marked CLOSED, and adjusted his glasses.

"You got any hair clippers?"

I put the panting dog down on the floor.

Castillo looked at me blankly.

"Clips, for the hair."

He grunted and then disappeared into the dark depths of the shop.

And then I placed the smell. My father had bought me a saxophone in a North Hollywood pawn shop when I was a kid. It didn't have all the parts and couldn't make all the notes, but I spent a summer and a good part of a winter loving the thing. The case it had come in smelled like Castillo's pawn shop.

Castillo returned, puffing from the burden of the box in his arms. He dropped the box on the counter and continued to pant heavily while I fished through the box of hair clippers till I found an old black one that looked as if it might still have teeth and wasn't too rusty.

"I'll take this one," I said.

"Two dollars," the old man said.

"What? It's not worth a quarter."

"Yesterday it was a quarter," Castillo said. "Today two bucks."

"What happened between yesterday and today?" I asked, watching Miguelito nose around behind a guitar-shaped box.

"Yesterday the police weren't looking for someone who looks like you," he said.

"I don't have any money . . ." I began, but Castillo spoke over me.

"Bicycle and the hat," he said.

"You can have them," I said.

"And the dog," Castillo added.

"You want that dog?"

"Si," said Castillo. "Para mi esposa."

"Okay. Give me the clipper to shave the dog. After I shave him, you can have him, but you have to throw in a shirt for me."

He handed me the clipper and came up with a small can of oil.

"I get the bike, the dog, and the clipper back," Castillo said readjusting his glasses as I oiled the clipper. "You get a shirt."

What the hell. I picked up the clipper and pulled Miguelito out from between the feet of a slightly chipped, full-size ceramic pig on which someone had written MONROE in nail polish. I shaved Miguelito, who simply watched with curiosity as I put the razor to his back.

The clipper wasn't bad. After a few false starts, I found a patch of fur that looked shorter than the rest and worked on in for a few seconds. Pay dirt. I could clearly see the lettering on the dog. I got down to bristle, read the names, and kept going. When I'd finished, Miguelito's back was exposed right down to his white skin.

"You got paper and a pencil?" I asked.

Castillo came up with them, and I copied what Lorna had written on her dog. It didn't make a hell of a lot of sense. Three names I didn't recognize—two men and a woman—a date, and a place: Cherokee, Texas.

"Without the hair he looks like a fat chihuahua," said Castillo. "I don't know if my wife wants a fat chihuahua. And who knows if we can get that ink washed off?"

"Then take him on trial," I said.

"Fifteen days," he said, making out a receipt. "You don't come back for him, my wife don't like him, I sell him. Fifteen days."

"Okay," I said, handing him the clipper, the hat, and the dog. In turn, he handed me a white shirt that looked a little large, but that was better than too small.

Miguelito lay there like a hairy cactus.

I took off my shirt, threw it to Castillo, and put on the white shirt. It wasn't too bad a fit.

"I can cover the dog so no one'll come around here and get curious about what's written on him till I get him home and wash him up," Castillo said, surveying the animal. "Got one of those blankets people put on greyhounds to race them. I'll show you."

He moved around the counter, went to a corner of the shop, and came up with a dusty box.

A few seconds later Miguelito's official number in gold was 9, and I was broke and on my way to look for a killer.

13

I tucked my shirt in and asked a pair of ladies carrying paper shopping bags how to get to the Opera—not the old Opera, but the one that was reopening.

"You mean the old barn where that guy got killed last week?"

"That's the place," I said.

"Dumb place to build a opera, you ask me," she said, shifting her bag from her right to left hand.

"Or anything else," said her friend. "Nobody goes there. Nothing around there. It's a dump."

After their critique and recommendations for urban renewal, they told me how to get to the Opera. It was about ten blocks away. I started out staying with the growing crowds, following a pride of young sailors for a few blocks, a gaggle of shoppers for another block.

It was somewhere near one in the afternoon when I hit the corner a block away from the Opera. I hid in a doorway and looked for the police. They weren't visible, but that didn't mean they weren't there. Reverend Souvaine's troops were out in force, about twenty of them. This was a big day. Dress rehearsal. Special guests, the press would be there.

The placards were bigger than ever. One announced: FIRST SACRILEGE. NOW MURDER. Another claimed: BUY A TICKET, HELP THE JAPS. Souvaine himself was not in sight. He'd show up for the crowds.

Across the street from where I was hiding, a rusting abandoned delivery van sat in a little weed-covered empty lot. The flecked dead paint on the side of the van indicated that it had once distributed Fleecy White Laundry Bleach, Little Boy Blue Bluing, and Little Bo-Peep Ammonia. Now it sat without tires, without front doors, and probably without engine, but with a better view of the San Francisco Metropolitan Opera Building than I had from the doorway. I moved out of the doorway, back down the block away from the street the Opera was on, crossed the street, and approached the van from behind. The back of the van had two doors; one was rusted shut, the other hung on one hinge. I climbed up and in and tried not to cut my hands on the bits of glass and pieces of metal left by kids or bums.

"Use Fleecy White, you'll find delight," I mumbled. "It's a peach of a bleach they say."

There were enough holes in the side of the van so I could see the front of the Opera. I was tired. I was hungry. My back let me know that it wasn't going to take much more of this without major complaints.

I watched for a while. Carpenters, painters, laborers, and guys with rolled-up blueprints under their arms came and went. It seemed as if the number of people working on the building had tripled and they were all moving fast to get the final touches done for the opening. The action inspired Souvaine's people, who marched with the step of the truly righteous. Sloane, Cynthia, and the widow Bertha were there shouting and urging the elderly to remain vigilant in case some Jap tried to sneak past them without reading their placards.

I could see Gunther's Daimler parked down the street in front of Stokowski's limo. Stokowski's driver leaned against the hood in full uniform, reading a newspaper and occasionally glancing over at the ancient army.

No cops, but they had to be there.

I sat for a few minutes, being careful not to get a splinter of something up my rear. Then, in one of the beams of light coming through the holes in the van, I found a discarded crushed can of Armour's Treet, the all-purpose meat. I used the jagged top of the can to pry at a small, already crumbling hole near my face. I managed under cover of the shouting in front of the Opera to make the hole big enough so I could see through it while sitting. Life was getting luxurious.

After about an hour, just as I was beginning to consider something risky, my break came. Two things happened at once. An overweight ancient woman carrying a placard reading ABANDON YOUR COUNTRY ALL YE WHO ENTER HERE suddenly collapsed. Cohorts screamed and abandoned their posts. Others continued to hold their banners high. Sloane knelt at the fallen warrior's side, and she and he were surrounded. At that same moment, Stokowski, Gunther, and Shelly came out the main door and started down the steps of the Opera.

Behind them a uniformed cop and Inspector Sunset came running down the steps in the direction of the fallen woman. From a doorway across the street another uniformed cop emerged, heading in their direction.

Shelly, sensing the need for his services, put a finger to his glasses and held up his cigar as he charged into the crowd, shouting, "Let me through, I'm a dentist."

The crowd parted and let him through. Gunther and Stokowski headed for the limousine, and I scrambled out of the back of the van. The limo was facing my direction. I hoped the driver wouldn't make a U-turn and move away from me.

Stokowski, who was wearing a pink shirt, narrow green tie,

gray suit, and what looked like tan suede shoes, glanced at the crowd, shook his shock-haired head, and moved with Gunther into the limousine. Sunset and the uniformed cops were breaking up the crowd of old people as I crossed the street and hid behind the corner of a small brick factory.

When the crowd cleared, the fat woman was sitting up and downing a bottle of Royal Crown Cola. She held it in two hands and took it like a baby getting its morning bottle. Shelly stood triumphant and looked around as if expecting applause. No one paid him any attention. The cops helped the fat lady up, and Shelly reluctantly ambled to the limousine. The second he got into it, the driver pulled away slowly, careful to avoid the bevy of the aged who had spilled into the street. The limo was about to turn the corner when I stepped into the street.

I waved my hands and the limo stopped. The back door opened and I scrambled in, tripping over Gunther's feet and landing on my face on the floor. The door closed and the limo pulled away down the street.

I rolled over on my back and found myself looking up at Stokowski. "There is something appropriately operatic about you and your entourage, Mr. Peters."

He reached down to help me to a sitting position and Shelly, sitting in the front seat next to the driver, peered down on me excitedly.

"You should have seen it, Toby," he said. "I just saved a woman's life."

"I'm proud of you, Shel," I said.

"Are you all right, Toby?" Gunther asked.

Even by his usual standards, Gunther was resplendent. His three-piece gray suit was neatly pressed, his tie new and silk, his face cleanly shaven, and there was a distinct smell of cologne in the air.

"I'm alive," I said. "How are you and Gwen getting along?"

I think Gunther blushed.

"A most accomplished young woman and a researcher of

the finest quality," he said. "We spent much of the night putting together the charts."

"Blammed her right above the heart," Shelly said to the driver, demonstrating a solid bang with his open palm. "Started to breathe right away."

"Can you ask your driver to pull over for a second?" I asked Stokowski.

Stokowski nodded and reached over me to touch the driver's shoulder. The car pulled over.

"I didn't kill her," I said.

"I did not think that you had," Stokowski said. "I've so informed the police. They are polite but not inclined to consider possibilities which will complicate their lives. It is easiest for them if you killed Miss Bartholomew."

"How long did she work for you?" I asked.

"A few weeks," he said. "Mr. Lundeen hired her to serve as my liaison for this engagement. Her work was adequate and her temperament erratic, which is not unusual for a former soprano."

"What do you know about her?" I went on.

Stokowski shrugged.

"Very little. As I said, she informed me that she had left a career, apparently not a greatly successful one, as a singer. She wished to remain close to musical life and because of her knowledge of opera had taken a variety of jobs in the area as they became available. I am very sorry, but I can't say that I am deeply grieved by what has happened to Miss Bartholomew. I am, however, deeply offended. The guilty must be punished."

"Like in an opera," Shelly offered.

"In opera, everyone is punished," said Stokowski.

I got off the floor, pulled down the jump seat, and sat facing Stokowski so I could see through the back window in case a patrol car headed our way.

"It might be a good idea to cancel the opening tonight," I said.

"That," he said, "I cannot do. It would be an act of cowardice.

There is destruction, horror, going on in Europe in this war. It cannot be forgotten. The feeling in our hearts must be respected. Music can play a part. I know it's only a small part, but it's a very important one because music can bring consolation, respite. It can remind us that with human life something exists of beauty to comfort and look forward to."

"Right," said Shelly excitedly. "It's like good dental hygiene."

"It is *not* like good dental hygiene," Gunther said precisely.

"Matter of opinion," Shelly said, beaming at us all.

"Mr. Peters," Stokowski said, "I assume you have joined us for a purpose. What can we do for you?"

"Short list," I said. "First, I need some money. The cops took my wallet."

"I am, unfortunately, carrying no cash," Stokowski said, turning up the cleanest palms I have ever seen.

Gunther came up with his wallet and handed me a pair of twenties.

"Next," I said, turning to Shelly, "I need to find a guy named Farkas, Snick Farkas. Skinny, about forty, carrying a blue shoulder bag. He's got a beard and should be wandering the streets around here. He's an opera buff. But he doesn't make much sense. I think he saw the person who killed Lorna Bartholomew."

"I'll find him," Shelly promised, clamping his unlit cigar in his teeth.

"He does not sound like an ideal witness," said Stokowski, with a sigh.

"Gunther, I've got some research for you."

I handed him the sheet of paper on which I'd written the message Lorna Bartholomew had painted on Miguelito. Gunther looked at it.

"Rance, Johnson, and Minnie," he read. "Cherokee, Texas. March 15, 1936. Those are characters in . . ."

"*La Fanciulla del West*. I know," I said. "See if you can find out what it means. Where's Jeremy?"

"With Miss Tenatti," replied Gunther.

"Anything else?" asked Stokowski. "I must eat and get back to rehearsal."

"I've got to get back and into the building," I said.

"You have a plan," said Stokowski.

"Your chauffeur and I are about the same size," I said.

"Ah," said Stokowski. "Charles, do you hear all this?"

"I hear," said the driver with a definite English accent.

"And . . . ?" Stokowski asked gently.

"There's an extra uniform in the trunk," said Charles.

"Good," I said. "I'll put it on. Charles, you get out here. I'll drive back, walk in as if the Maestro forgot something. Shelly, you wait till I've been inside for two minutes, and then drive back and pick up Charles. I'll get the uniform back later."

Charles nodded.

"Anything else?" Stokowski asked.

"I could use something to eat," I said.

"Take my lunch," said Charles, handing me a paper bag. "I'll pick up a hot dog."

"Charles, you'll lunch with Mr. Wherthman, Dr. Minck, and me," said Stokowski. Sounded like a generous offer, but I had the feeling Gunther would wind up with the check.

"You might get in trouble for this, Maestro," I said, getting out of the limo.

"Trouble is not unknown to me," Stokowski said. "There are those who say I have courted controversy and both bedded and wed her."

"Be cautious, Toby," Gunther said.

"Am I ever anything but? Let's meet in Lundeen's office at seven." I moved to the rear of the car.

I could hear Shelly's voice as the trunk popped open.

"See his teeth, Stoki? Nice, huh? My doing? A year of work."

"That's admirable," Stokowski said.

I opened a box in the trunk that looked right. It was. A freshly pressed uniform. I looked around for someplace to change. The street was deserted but the sun was high and bright. Hell.

I took off my clothes and started putting on the uniform. I got it on without interruption.

"Good fit," Charles said.

He was standing next to me, his cap off. He was older than I thought. He wiped his brow with a handkerchief. His hair was curly, short, and white. His skin pinkish.

"Thanks," I said.

"When the war started," Charles said, "the Maestro moved to Columbia Records. One of the first things he recorded was 'God Bless America' and 'The Star Spangled Banner' coupled with the Pledge of Allegiance to the Flag. I was in the orchestra. Bass viol."

"What happened?" I asked.

Charles pulled off his right driving glove and revealed a hand with a thumb and two fingers.

"Went back to England," he said. "London bomb patrol. War turned me into a driver. Got a son in the RAF and another on bomb patrol. Truth is, Stoki's not that much fond of the British. His mum was Irish, but he made an exception in my case. Got me a job driving here in Frisco. He asks for me whenever he comes to town. The Maestro's trying his best. I'd hate to see something happen to him."

"Nothing will happen. I look okay?" I asked.

"Smashing," he said with a smile, moving to the curb and pulling a newspaper from his pocket.

I got in the driver's seat, pulled the cap over my eyes, made a U-turn and headed back for the Opera. It took no more than three minutes. The boys and girls of the Church of the Enlightened Patriots were back in business, even the fat lady, though she no longer had her bottle of RC and was sitting on the steps conducting the camp meeting rather than participating.

I pulled up to the curb, got out, winked at Stokowski, who gave me a small salute and said, "For some reason, I am hearing the Brahms First Symphony, which I have always found plaintive."

"Shelly, find Snick Farkas," I said. "Gunther, I'm counting on you to find out what happened in Cherokee, Texas."

"I'm on the job," said Shelly.

Gunther simply nodded.

I turned and started up the steps, head down. I got through the main doors and out of the corner of my eyes spotted Sunset in a corner, showing a uniformed cop who looked about twelve the proper stance to take against a right-handed pitcher. Sunset glanced over at me as I walked quickly toward the corridor. Then he went back to his batting clinic.

I went through a side entrance to the auditorium. A crew of women was dusting the seats and sweeping the aisles. On stage, about twenty men and women in overalls were putting up a Japanese house set. No Vera. No Lundeen. No Passacaglia. A few musicians were in the orchestra pit adjusting their instruments, playing a few bars.

I moved to the stage, cap still covering my eyes, went up the steps, and moved toward the back of the stage.

"Hold it," a voice I recognized called from the rear of the auditorium.

I stopped and turned, pretending to shield my eyes from the light to cover my face.

"What the hell you trying to pull?" called Sergeant Preston.

He stepped out of the shadows under the balcony and pointed at me.

It had been a good try but I hadn't made it. I considered running, but decided I was twenty years too late to make that a reasonable option. I reached up to take off the cap as Preston took another step forward yelling, "You, take that cap off!"

Since I was obviously in the process of doing just that, I paused. It was enough of a pause to realize that he wasn't pointing at me but past me, at a workman about my size in overalls and a painter's cap.

"Get out of the way," Preston said, this time to me.

I stepped out of the way. The workman took his cap off. He was Oriental.

"All right. All right, put it back on," Preston said. "Jesus, I should have been the second-rate crooner my mother never wanted me to be. And you," he went on, pointing directly at me. "Stokowski says he wants you to hurry up."

I nodded, touched the brim of my cap, and hurried into the wings.

Jeremy was standing, arms folded, leaning against the wall next to Vera's dressing room. He glanced in my direction. His eyes seemed focused on a distant planet, but he took me in.

"Are you all right, Toby?" he asked.

"How'd you know it was me?" I asked, stepping in front of him.

Jeremy shrugged.

"The walk, the change in pressure on the backs of my hands, a sense of you."

"Touch of the poet," I said.

"It's there for all of us to take," he said. "It is the feminine within each of us we fear to explore, even women."

"I'll take your word for it," I said. "What happened to Ortiz?"

"Following his hospitalization, he faces extradition to Mexico for a variety of crimes," said Jeremy.

"How's your back, where he bit you?" I asked.

"I'm directing my energy to it. It will heal."

"Good. Vera all right?"

"She is fine," he said. "The tenor is in there with her. There are police in all directions."

"I know," I said. "If they come by, keep them out if you can."

"I can," said Jeremy with a gentle smile.

"I know," I said, knocking at Vera's door.

Her "Come in" had an undertone of urgency. I went in and closed the door.

Passacaglia had Vera pinned to the wall. They didn't recognize me.

"Get out," said Passacaglia.

"Stay," cried Vera. "Call the big man."

"Out," Passacaglia insisted. "You are intruding on a lovers' quarrel."

I stepped forward and put my hand on Passacaglia's arm.

"Old man," he said. "You are about to be embarrassed."

I took off my cap, put it on Vera's head, and showed Passacaglia my face.

"Toby," Vera said with relief.

Passacaglia pushed away from the wall and hit me across the bridge of what was left of my nose with the back of his hand. It was a reasonably powerful clout. I didn't reach up to check for blood. I didn't want to mess up Charles' uniform.

"Killer," hissed Passacaglia. "Killer of women."

I grinned and took a step toward him. He backed up.

"Do not hit," he warned, with one hand up. "Do not touch my face or my diaphragm."

I pushed his hand out of the way. He tried another backhand. I caught that with my shoulder and threw a short right to his stomach. He doubled over. Vera gasped behind me. Passacaglia held one hand on his stomach and threw another backhand at my face. I stepped back and slapped at his face. He turned away from the slap and it caught him on the neck. He went down gasping.

"I told you no face, no diaphragm," he moaned. "Are you deaf?"

I helped him to his feet and looked at Vera. The chauffeur's cap sat at a rakish angle on her head. She looked cute as hell. I told her. She touched my cheek.

"My throat," croaked Passacaglia. "I . . . you fool. I won't be able to sing tonight."

"You'll recover," I said.

"Not in time," he said, "You've damaged a delicate instrument."

His voice did have a sandpaper rasp.

"You sound better," I said.

"I'll sue you," he said, pointing a finger at me.

"Fear is striking my very soul," I said. "The police are looking for me for murder and you threaten me for temporarily cancelling a tenor?"

"Remorse," he tried, looking at himself in Vera's mirror. "Contrition. Apology. Is this too much to ask?"

"I'm sorry," I said. "I couldn't think of anyplace else to hit you."

"The shoulder," he said, voice going quickly, pointing to his shoulder. "Or you could have kicked me in the ass. Peters, you may be assured that this incident ensures that there is no way we can ever be friends or that I can even be cordial to you. I am leaving."

His voice was just about gone now.

"Martin," Vera said. "I'm sorry, but you did . . ."

Passacaglia had one hand on the doorknob, the other at his neck. I knew where he was heading.

"Martin," I said. "We may not be friends, but we are going to make a deal. You don't tell the cops I'm here, and I don't make a call to your wife and tell her you've been trying to do some extra rehearsals with Vera."

Passacaglia sneered in my direction.

"Traitor. Robber. Scoundrel. Imposter," he rasped and left, slamming the door.

"I think the exit line was from the chorus of *Gianni Schicchi*," Vera said.

"Puccini?"

"Yes."

I kissed her. She tasted like the memory of lilacs.

"Maestro Stokowski will be upset," Vera said, in my arms. "We have no understudies."

"Let's see what we can do about it," I said, leading her to the door, taking my cap back and planting it on my head.

"Which way did he go?" I asked Jeremy.

Jeremy nodded to the left, down the corridor, toward an exit sign.

"Let's find big John," I said, and led the way to the stairway just outside the backstage door leading inside the auditorium. There was no one in the darkened corridor. The three of us went up the stairs and made our way to Lundeen's office. We didn't hear anything inside.

I stepped back and Vera knocked.

"Come in," Lundeen boomed, the weight of the opera on his broad shoulders.

He was not alone in the room. The Reverend Souvaine stood next to the broad desk facing Lundeen, who stood behind it. They were almost eyeball to eyeball—teeth, fists, and stomachs clenched.

"Now get out," Lundeen shouted at Souvaine, who had the best of the moment sartorially. The reverend was wearing a near-white Palm Beach suit with a ruffled white shirt and a powder blue tie. Lundeen was wearing baggy slacks and a sloppy brown wool sweater too large even for him.

"I came in peace to talk reason and righteousness," bellowed Souvaine, without looking back at us.

I hid behind Jeremy, which was easy to do.

"You came to dictate pious lies!" shouted Lundeen. "You came like a Wagnerian Nazi in the night to stifle art."

"At least," said Souvaine, "we agree about Wagner."

"Out," Lundeen said, his hand sending a pile of charts flying across the room.

"If you try to open," said Souvaine, standing erect, "God will surely strike you with the lightning staff of the flag of the nation which he loves above all others."

"Fool!" bellowed Lundeen, coming around the table. "Mixer of metaphors!"

"Overweight blasphemer," said Souvaine softly.

Jeremy stepped between the two men, leaving me exposed. I pulled the cap farther over my eyes and moved behind Vera. Lundeen tried to reach past Jeremy to get at Souvaine, who stood his ground.

"Pompous swindler!" cried Lundeen.

"Cartoon," said Souvaine.

"Fart!" screamed Lundeen.

"Fart?" echoed Souvaine. "Is that the height of your creativity?"

Lundeen growled and pleaded with Jeremy. "Let me kill him. Just a little."

"You have my prayers, my pity, and my warning," said Souvaine, who paused at the door and turned to Jeremy. "And you will suffer both the wrath of the Lord and the law for the unprovoked attack you made on the Reverend Ortiz. 'The Lord is far from the wicked; but he heareth the prayer of the righteous.' Proverbs Fifteen, Verse Twenty-eight."

"It's Verse Twenty-nine," Jeremy corrected. "Verse Twenty-eight is 'The heart of the righteous studieth to answer, but the mouth of the wicked poureth out evil.'"

"You are wrong about the verse," said Souvaine, his face turning pink.

I wanted to put up the forty bucks in my pocket on Jeremy's being right, but I kept my mouth shut and Souvaine went out, slamming the door. Lundeen moved back behind his desk and sat with his head in his hands.

"Peters," he said without looking up. "What are you doing here? The police are fluttering around the place like bats."

"Great disguise I've got here," I said, taking off my cap. "Only the police don't recognize me."

"I'm an actor," said Lundeen. "Or I was. I can see through a costume, a mask."

With that he looked up at the three of us and swept his hand in an arc. "All these papers," he said. "That little man and Gwen spent the night. And what was the result? Everyone still has an alibi. . . . Listen to me. I'm using dialogue from cheap radio shows. That's what my life has come to. Everyone has an alibi for either the workman's death or the attacks on Lorna. No one was unseen by someone else for at least one of the incidents. The more incidents we get, the more charts we do and the less sense it makes."

"Maybe it was more than one person," Vera said.

"Ah," sighed Lundeen, pointing at her. "Suddenly sopranos can think. Yes, it's a conspiracy. I'm beginning to agree with you."

He laughed without enthusiasm.

"Let's see," he said. "Souvaine, Raymond, and I have conspired with the police. Everyone is in on it, perhaps even Lorna, who was not killed by our Mr. Peters but committed suicide because she couldn't stand the guilt and the complication."

"Lundeen," I said.

"And," Lundeen went on, "Gwen tells me she is leaving after *Butterfly,* assuming we actually get to perform. I think she is running off to Los Angeles with your German midget."

"Gunther's Swiss," I corrected.

"Swiss," sighed Lundeen. "This is as bizarre as a Mozart opera."

"It gets worse," I said.

Lundeen looked at me and went silent.

"There is nothing worse," he said after a moment.

"Martin Passacaglia can't sing Pinkerton tonight," I said.

"They killed him, too?" Lundeen's mouth fell open to reveal a limp red tongue.

"I hit him in the neck," I admitted.

"You . . ." he began.

". . . hit him in the neck. He was mauling Vera," I said.

"Mauling Vera," Lundeen repeated, looking at Jeremy.

Jeremy had no answer.

"Toby has an idea," Vera said softly.

"You are a tenor who knows the part of Pinkerton?" he asked calmly, folding his hands on the desk.

"No, but you're a baritone who knows the part," I said.

"I . . . me . . . sing Pinker . . . You're mad," Lundeen said, suddenly standing.

"You've got a better idea?" I asked, moving to a chair and sitting. I pulled Charles' lunch out of my pocket, opened it, and fished out a sandwich. I think it was Spam and ketchup. I didn't care. I was hungry.

"I haven't sung on stage in years," he said. "And it's not written for . . ."

"You know the role, Mr. Lundeen," Vera said. "And this is only the dress rehearsal. By opening, Martin will be fine."

"If you don't go on, you may be kissing *Butterfly* good-bye," I said.

"The Maestro would never . . ." Lundeen began.

"I think he will," I said. "He wants this to go on. He's a patriot, remember."

"A patriot who is getting a generous fee for his services. The costume would never fit me," he tried, his eyes on Jeremy.

"Call in your costume people," said Jeremy. "I'll help. Sewing is a meditation with which I am familiar."

"It will be a disaster," Lundeen protested, throwing charts and graphs on the floor.

"Consider the alternative," said Jeremy.

Lundeen stopped ranting and appeared to consider the alternative.

"Yes," he said.

I finished the sandwich and went to work on Charles the Chauffeur's apple.

"That's settled," I said.

"Perhaps," said Lundeen, "but there is more to this hoary tale."

He reached into his pocket and pulled out a crumpled piece of paper. He handed the paper to Jeremy, who handed it to me. I uncrumpled it and read:

If she sings tonight, at midnight she will be the third to die.

Erik

"It was pinned to my office door when I arrived this morning," Lundeen said.

"What does it say?" Vera said, reaching for the note.

I considered keeping it from her but it was her life, her choice. I held it out and she took it. She read it quickly and then read it again.

"Do you think he . . . ?"

"I don't know, Vera," I said. "But you sing and we'll see that no one touches you."

"Can you guarantee that, Toby?" she asked, her large brown eyes looking down at me.

"No."

"I'll sing," she said.

"There's a good chance we'll have the Phantom before the performance," I said. "Gunther's following up a lead I got from Miguelito."

"The dog?" Lundeen asked.

"The dog."

Lundeen shook his head in disbelief.

"Ruined," he said. "Vera, we must get on stage. We must rehearse. I'll have to go over the blocking."

"Jeremy," I said. "Stick with her."

Jeremy blinked once to show me that he understood. I left the room, closing the door behind me. I could hear Lundeen's voice through the closed door calling on the phone for the costume shop.

Something was bothering me, but I had too many pieces to put together.

14

Cap back on my head, stomach not quite full but satisfied, I made my way back to old Raymond's tower. He wasn't there. The door to the room was off its hinges and the furniture, what was left of it after Ortiz and Jeremy's best-out-of-one match, was one step away from kindling.

I looked around but there was nothing much to find. No clues to Raymond's past, present, or future. I gave it up and headed back down the steps. I hit the first level down and heard a creak from behind. I looked up in time to see a barrel tottering at the edge of the top step. Someone was behind it, but I couldn't see more than a dark shape.

"Hold it," I said, but he didn't hold it. He let it go and it started klomping down. The steps were narrow, the landing a few feet across. I jumped down two steps hoping the barrel would break up or stop at the landing. It didn't. It did pop open and begin to spit out nails.

I tore down the stairs pursued by the barrel and a laugh above me that I didn't like at all. I got halfway down the second narrow flight and tripped, which probably saved my life. I fell on my shoulder and tumbled faster than the barrel. I went flat at the next landing and tried to hide under the bottom stair. The barrel bounced and sailed about an inch over my head, crashing past, raining nails.

I got to my knees and touched the parts of me that might be broken. I was still operating. Charles' uniform was dead, punctuated by flying nails and splintered stairs, but I wasn't. I was damned mad. The laughter above me had stopped, but I went up. I was hurting, but the hell with it.

"Laugh, you clown," I shouted. "I've got one for you that'll put you in stitches."

I could hear the barrel come to a crash somewhere. I stopped. Silence. And then the sound of footsteps above. I went up the steps two or three at a time. Whoever was above me was scrambling now. I kept coming. When I made it to the landing in front of Raymond's sanctuary, I stopped. There was no one in the room, no place to hide, no place to go.

Listen, I told myself. Don't even breathe. Listen. Out on the bay a foghorn blew. I waited and then heard a creak to my right, near the window in Raymond's room. I moved to the dirty window and saw that it was open a crack. I pushed and leaned out in time to see a cape disappearing around a corner of the tower. If he could do it, so could I. I climbed out the window, found a foothold, a narrow brick-width stone ledge, and started after the Phantom. I held tight to the bricks, kissed them, and didn't look down, but I knew down was a long way off. A piece of ledge cracked under my foot. I told myself to take it easy. I turned the corner. No one was there. I kept inching and found another open window. I was about to plunge through when a flying bust of some Greek came sailing past my nose. I ducked, holding onto the window ledge, expecting someone to cut off my fingers. Instead, I heard footsteps moving away from the window. I went over the edge and back into the building, tumbling onto my side. I sat listening, letting my eyes get used to the darkness again, and then I got up and went after the sound of heels hitting wooden floors. I didn't know where the hell he was going, but we weren't going down. My hands touched curtains, metal rails. Sounds echoed and the guy in front of me hummed.

"You want singing?" I shouted. "I'll sing."

I bellowed out "The Love Bug Will Get You If You Don't Watch Out" and what I could remember of "Minnie the Moocher" and bumped into a door. I shut up, found the handle, stepped through, and almost fell a hundred feet to the stage below. I teetered on the edge of a small platform beyond the door, looking for something to grab. I was reaching for a rope and going forward when he pushed me from behind. My hands caught one of the ropes and held. I turned my head for an instant to see a flash of cape as the door I'd tripped through closed.

I considered calling for help. Someone might hear me, but I didn't think anyone could get up here before my grip slipped. I started down the rope, not knowing where it would end. I found out fast. I ran out of rope with a forty-foot fall below me. The red velvet stage curtains were touching my face. I grabbed for a fold, caught it with one hand, and did the same with the other. There was nothing to climb, nothing to use, and not much strength left in my fingers.

I closed my eyes, felt my stomach go, and a musty breeze brush my face. I had time to think that I had either let go of the curtain and was falling, which I didn't believe, or that the curtain had torn from my weight and was falling with me, which I did believe. I stopped with a jerk, lost my grip, and fell backward on the stage.

When I opened my eyes, I found myself looking up at Raymond Griffith.

"That is one dangerous way to have yourself a good time," he said. "I can tell you that. I didn't let you down you'd have been creamy mushroom soup."

I sat up and looked at him. He was bedecked in overalls and a clean shirt. A cardboard suitcase sat next to him.

"You are going somewhere?" I asked, trying to stand but shaking too much.

"Distant horizon," he said. "Time I moved on. Forty years is enough to spend in one place, my mother used to say."

"Why would your mother say that?" I asked.

"Maybe she said four years," he answered with a shrug.

"I don't want to be ungrateful, Raymond," I said. "But I'm afraid I'll have to ask you to stay till after tonight's performance."

"I've seen *Madame Butterfly*," he said. "Think I saw the U.S. of A. premiere. Didn't like it much. I've seen a lot."

"I'll bet you have," I said. "Ever see *La Fanciulla del West*?"

Raymond's idiot yokel mask dropped. "Sorry you saved me?"

"No," he answered in a voice I'd never heard from him. "Sorry you ask too many questions."

He picked up his suitcase, turned, and headed for the far wings.

"Hold it," I called, rising on wobbly legs.

"Peters," he said, "I'm not staying around to get myself killed or spend the remainder of my life behind steel bars. I've spent my life playing everything from minstrel shows to third-rate opera. It's kept me alive, and that's the way I want to stay. I signed on for this role, but the play's getting too serious for me."

"Cherokee, Texas," I said.

"You've got all the pieces," Raymond said.

I took a couple of unsteady steps toward him when the door at the back of the auditorium started to open. Instead of crossing the stage, I rolled behind the fallen curtain and duck-walked to the wings. I looked back to see Preston, Sunset, and a pair of uniformed cops moving down the aisle toward the stage. I got up, took off my shoes, and ran into the darkness.

Vera's dressing room was close by. I went for it. The door was open. The lights were out. I left them that way and felt along the wall for the curtained-off closet to the right. I pushed back the curtain, went in, closed the curtain, and sat on the floor behind hanging clothes. I felt around on the floor and found a plaster head with a wig on it. I moved the head carefully, took off Charles's frayed jacket, put it on the floor under my head, and with a groan curled into an aching ball.

I fell asleep. I don't remember the dream very well. Koko was there. So was Winston Churchill. Raymond was dressed as a Japanese cowboy. That I remember. Then the sound of voices awoke me and then the light went on.

It wasn't exactly bright in the closet, but I could see Raymond clearly. He sat in the corner about three feet away, looking at a spot just above my head, his suitcase in his lap. He was definitely dead. I could tell that even without the sword sticking out of his stomach.

". . . so Osa Johnson said," a woman's voice came as I tried to quietly sit up, doing my best to ignore or overcome the pain. "She said, 'I'll bet the cannibal natives are wondering why we're killing so many Japs. They know we can't possibly eat all of them.'"

I made it to something resembling a sitting position.

"That's very funny, Gwen," Vera said.

"Actually," answered Gwen, "I thought it was when I read it, but it just seems a bit stupid now."

I could see the out lines of the two women against the cloth curtains draping the closet. Vera appeared to be sitting at her dressing table.

"It's all right," said Vera. "I appreciate your helping me. I . . . we'd better get ready. My first-act costume and wig are in the closet."

I was propped in one corner, the dead Raymond in the other when Gwen threw back the curtain and pushed the clothes back to reveal us.

"You know what time it is?" I asked.

Gwen looked at us and gasped. Vera heard her, turned in

her chair, saw me and the sword sticking out of Raymond, and screamed.

A knock at the dressing room door. Vera jumped from her chair, closed the closet curtain, and said, "Come in."

The door opened and I heard Sunset's voice.

"You all right?"

"I was rehearsing," said Vera. She went up and down the scales to prove her point.

"You're all right?" Sunset repeated.

"Fine," she said. "I've got to get made up and dressed. Mr. Butler, could you stay and give Gwen a hand with my costume?"

"I'll be outside," said Sunset.

The door closed. Footsteps. The cloth curtain was pulled back and I looked up at Vera, Jeremy, and Gwen.

"I did not do it," I said, nodding at Raymond. "I came in here to hide and fell asleep. When I woke up, there he was."

Jeremy helped me up.

"I believe you," said Vera. "Can we . . . I'd rather not look. . . ."

I stepped out of the closet and Gwen closed the curtain.

"What time is it?" I asked.

"Just before six," Gwen said, looking at her wristwatch. "Dress rehearsal is at eight."

"We can't leave him in there," Vera said, pointing at the closet.

"Call the cops and I'll be up for two murders, and spending the night with Detective Sunset, who would probably use my head for batting practice," I said.

"I'm afraid you can't get out of here, Toby," Jeremy said.

I looked around the room. There wasn't much to see.

"Dress rehearsal is at eight," said Gwen again, looking at the closed curtain.

"Maestro Stokowski is not pleased with the compromise of using John Lundeen as Pinkerton," said Jeremy.

"It looks as if Martin Passacaglia will be all right for opening night," said Vera, taking Gwen's hand. "If not, the Maestro found a tenor in Los Angeles who can be down here in a day."

"Wouldn't the new guy have to rehearse, block, whatever?" I asked.

"It helps," said Vera, "but featured singers sometimes come in the afternoon of a performance, go through simple blocking, and then do it. It's not the best way, but it's done."

"Looks like I'm done, too," I said.

"No," said Vera, touching my cheek. "I think I have an idea. Gwen, we need makeup, costumes, wigs, and men."

"That's always been my philosophy," Gwen agreed.

Vera explained her plan. I'd heard better, but it wasn't bad.

"Jeremy," I said. "Gunther and Shelly are in Lundeen's office. Can you get them down here?"

Jeremy nodded and moved to the door. Gwen went with him. I went back behind the curtains while they opened the door and went out. When I heard Vera lock it, I came out.

Vera's hands were folded. She was looking at Raymond. I closed the curtains.

"That sword," she said. "It's the one I'm supposed to use in the last act to commit hari-kari."

"They'll have a backup," I said, moving to her side and putting an arm around her.

"The police," she said. "Maybe they'll think I killed . . ."

"We'll get Raymond out of here," I assured her.

"I think this Erik is really going to try to kill me," she said with a shiver that went through us both.

"You want to have Stokowski call the whole thing off?"

She went rigid. Her back went straight.

"No," she said. "If I quit, if there is no performance, no opera, then Lorna and that poor man will have died for nothing."

"Sounds like the war," I said.

"Perhaps it is," she agreed, moving to her dressing table and sitting.

I leaned over and kissed her.

"Did he bleed on my wig?"

"No."

"Why . . . who killed that poor man?"

"The why I know," I said. "He knew who killed Lorna and who's been playing Phantom. He wasn't a harmless old bat. He was an actor hired, blackmailed, or bribed into helping our Erik, but he didn't count on killing."

"Now he's dead," she said. "These are very trying circumstances in which to give a performance."

"I'll give you that," I said, grimacing as I leaned against the dressing table.

"You're in pain?" She touched my cheek.

"Maybe just a little," I admitted.

It was hard to carry on a tender conversation with a skewered corpse in the closet and the police outside the door looking for me. Luckily, Gwen came knocking within fifteen minutes.

"It's me," she said. "Are you decent? The policeman is being kind enough to help me with the costumes."

I knew a hint when I heard one. I went back in with Raymond. He was still dead. The door opened and Gwen said. "Right over there."

"Sure," said Sunset. Then he left and the door was closed and locked.

When I came out this time, Gwen was piling wigs and a big leather box on the dressing table. A stack of silly-looking costumes was on the floor.

Another knock at the door. This time it was Jeremy, Shelly, and Gunther. When the door was locked, Gunther moved to Gwen's side and patted her hand. Shelly looked at the room in confusion; Jeremy leaned back against the door, arms folded.

"What's going on?" Shelly inquired, adjusting his glasses.

I moved to the closet and pushed open the curtain.

"I think he's dead, Toby," Shelly said seriously.

"I think so, Shel," I agreed.

"I don't care to be around dead people," said Shelly, beads

of sweat now clear on his forehead. "Especially ones with big knives in them."

"None of us do," I said, closing the curtain.

"Why couldn't we meet upstairs where there aren't any dead people?" Shelly asked. "This place looks like the stateroom scene in *A Night at the Opera*."

"That's just what it is, Shel," I said.

Vera explained her plan. We were all going to get dressed as Japanese, complete with wigs and makeup. Even Raymond. Then at curtain time we'd all come streaming out and sweep right past Sunset and his cavalry.

"I don't like it," said Shelly, "I don't look Japanese."

"You will when Gwen and I finish with you," said Vera. "We haven't much time."

Finding costumes for Shelly, me, and Raymond proved easy. Jeremy and Gunther were the big problems. Gwen managed a transformation of Gunther, but Jeremy proved too great a task. They gave up.

While we dressed, I got the information that would make sense out of most of what was going on.

Shelly had found Snick Farkas in front of the Opera after looking around the neighborhood for hours. Farkas had camped on the steps, five-dollar bill in hand, watching Souvaine's troops while he waited for someone to tell him how to buy a ticket. Shelly had told him there were no tickets for the dress rehearsal but he could get him in. Farkas had been more than happy to come.

"He's sitting in the back row," said Shelly, shifting his cigar stub so Gwen could apply makeup to his cheeks.

Gunther's information was even more valuable and came in a rectangular envelope he handed to me.

"You will find in the envelope the playbill for the performance of *La Fanciulla del West* on March 15, 1936," said Gunther. "However, the event never came to pass. I called the office of the newspaper in Cherokee, Texas, which I got from the information operator. A woman named Esther Trosow, who serves as editor, read to me the news item of that day. It seems there was an unfortunate incident: A person who played a bartender in the production was killed. The company was gone before the sheriff, a man named Pyle, could investigate fully. Citizens were upset that they did not get their money back."

"How'd you get this?" I asked, opening the envelope and trying not to wrinkle the rubber bald pate Vera had placed on my head.

"Miss Trosow informed me that a gentleman from Cherokee who had been manager with the Wild Bill Hickok Opera House had moved to Santa Rosa and that he might have more information. With Miss Trosow's help, I located the man, who informed me that he had kept both the clippings and the playbill for the event because it marked the end of any attempt to bring opera to Cherokee, Texas."

"Did you look at this?" I asked Gunther, who was adjusting the sleeves on his tiny costume.

"I did," he said.

"What?" cried Shelly, turning his head and dropping a clump of ashes on his costume.

"For starters," I said. "The part of Minnie was sung by . . ."

"Supposed to be sung by," Gunther corrected.

"Supposed to be sung by," I amended, "Lorna Bartlett."

"Lorna Bartholomew?" Shelly asked.

I didn't answer.

"A man named Roger Griffith was supposed to play three parts in the opera," I went on. We all looked at the dead Raymond, who, propped in the corner, sword now removed from his chest and placed neatly in his sash, looked like John Carradine as a transvestite.

A knock at the door and a voice. "Ten minutes to dress rehearsal."

"Thank you," called Vera, who no longer looked like Vera but a white-faced Japanese with a pile of dark hair.

"What else?" asked Shelly, admiring himself in the mirror. He looked like an Oriental version of Fiorello La Guardia.

"There's a picture here," I said. "Not a good one, but a picture from the Cherokee *Daily Indian*, a picture of guy who was supposed to sing the lead in *La Fanciulla del West.*"

I passed the picture around. No one said a word. I dropped it back in the envelope and stuffed the package in my purple kimono.

Another knock and the voice. "On stage."

"Let's do it," I said.

Jeremy lifted Raymond Griffith's body with one hand and I moved behind him. Gwen, not in costume, was at the rear of the parade. Vera led us out the door. We all pretended to exercise our voices.

People, some in costume, some carrying instruments, were scurrying around. Sunset, Preston, and uniformed police were standing off to the side examining faces. Preston looked directly at me. I opened my mouth and let out a falsetto "Fa, Fa, Fa," and kept in the middle of the crowd.

We moved onto the stage. The curtain was down. There was a thronelike chair in one corner of the Japanese home set. Jeremy and I placed the dead Raymond in the chair, and I asked Jeremy to find Farkas and sit with him. Jeremy nodded and left the stage. Gwen squeezed Gunther's hand and moved off.

"The first scene," Vera said to me, "is supposed to be between Pinkerton and Cio-cio-san's maid. There's a garden set in front of the curtain. Goro would normally come out a bit later, but Maestro Stokowski has taken some creative liberties with the story, so . . ."

"Got it," I said. "You going to be okay?"

"Yes." Vera nodded.

And she was off. Members of the chorus, all dressed as Japanese, quietly found places on the set. Some of them looked at Gunther, Shelly, and me as if we were extras lost from a road show of *The Mikado*.

Through the curtain, the overture began. It sounded loud, strong, sure to me. Gunther pulled me down to him to whisper, "He's improvising. Stokowski is improvising with Puccini."

"Sounds okay to me," I said.

"But," posed Gunther, adjusting his kimono, "is the proper role of the musician to render the composer's work faithfully or to use it as a point of departure for his own creativity?"

"Beats hell out of me, Gunther," I admitted, trying to work out how I was going to unmask a killer and get the police off my back.

"It is a conundrum," said Gunther.

I moved to the curtain and parted it just enough to see Stokowski, eyes closed in concentration, whipping his hands frantically. Behind him I could see an audience of about a hundred for the dress rehearsal. I couldn't see Jeremy and Farkas in the rear, but I was counting on them being there.

The overture stopped and Vera began to sing.

She sounded light, happy, a Japanese song bird singing in Italian. Lundeen came in. He didn't sound bad either, but I had the feeling he wasn't hitting the upper end of the role.

When the curtain came up for the wedding party, the chorus sang, Gunther and I mouthed, and Raymond sat dead. No problems. Lundeen strolled the stage, smiling in a tight blue, ersatz navy uniform with brass buttons. He was sweating. As he passed without recognizing me, I whispered, "Ever play Samson?"

The smile fell from his face and he stopped walking and looked at me.

"How about Johnson in *La Fanciulla del West*?" I tried pulling the envelope out of my kimono to remove the newspaper photograph of Lundeen, looking thirty pounds thinner and two to four murders lighter. I held it up for the baritone to see. He turned into a tower of sweat and missed his cue.

There was a long pause. The orchestra stopped playing. Vera resang her line. Someone coughed.

"Giancarlo," Stokowski's voice came. "This is a dress rehearsal. You have just been given a cue. There is an audience waiting, an orchestra waiting."

"I . . ." Lundeen began, turning to the audience.

"Snick," I shouted. "You ever see this man before?"

From the back of the auditorium came the wavering voice of Snick Farkas. "*Samson et Dalila*, City of the Angels in 1938, '39, something like that."

"Mr. Peters," Stokowski said above the sudden hum and rising of the crowd.

"Anyplace else?" I asked, stepping to the front of the stage.

"Yesterday," came Farkas' voice. "Going into that building you hit me in front of with the car. Just before you went in."

"Mr. Peters," Stokowski repeated. "Am I to understand that you are about to eliminate my second Pinkerton of the day?"

"Looks that way, Maestro," I said.

"And we are to understand," Stokowski said, playing his role perfectly, "that Mr. Lundeen killed Miss Bartholomew?"

"Right," I said.

I could feel rather than see Preston and Sunset coming out of the wings in my direction.

"He also killed Raymond Griffith," I said, pointing to the corpse on the throne.

That stopped Preston and Sunset, who looked at the dead man.

"And Mr. Peters," Stokowski said, arms folded, lifting his chin at me, playing the perfect straight man. "Why did Giancarlo do these things?"

"My guess is he wants this opera to fail," I said. "He pulled this scam on a smaller level back in Texas seven years ago. Combination of insurance scam and overselling to backers. I think someone objected to it then and got killed."

"Madness," cried Lundeen, arms out, walking around the stage, asking the audience for sympathy.

"Nope," I said, pulling the bald pate off my head and scratching where it itched. "You were in it with Lorna and Griffith. I think she changed her mind when she decided maybe you weren't just faking attacks on her. Gunther and I went over all the information on where people said they were when Wyler the plasterer died, when I was attacked, and when Lorna was attacked twice. You, Lorna, and Griffith always covered for each other. But you overcovered. All three of you said you saw a guy with a cape climbing up the scaffolding before the carpenter died. But you were seen inside the auditorium just before the death of the plasterer. I'll bet the poor guy just fell and you made up the Phantom story."

"But Lorna . . ." Lundeen pleaded.

Preston and Sunset had stopped now. Their attention was turned to Lundeen.

"Funny thing," I said. "When I found her body in her apartment, she was covered with bruises, but not on her neck. Her neck was untouched, no marks. Only hours before, the neck was bruised and red from the Phantom's attack on her.

"But there was no attack on Lorna Bartholomew. She rubbed makeup on her neck and came running up the stairs screaming. After the attack she wore a scarf around her neck."

"This is ridiculous," Lundeen said to Stokowski and the audience.

"It has the ring of dramatic authenticity," said Stokowski, looking to his orchestra for confirmation. They nodded in agreement. The audience was discussing the situation in small groups.

"Should be easy enough to check your books, contractors, donors, to see if you stand to profit by the opera failing," I said to Lundeen. "Gunther can do it with Gwen and . . ."

Lundeen looked at me at stage center, Preston and Sunset stage right, Shelly and Gunther stage left, and the orchestra and audience out in front and made his decision. He pushed Vera out of the way and leaped into the orchestra pit, crashing noisily through a kettle drum. Musicians scurried out of the way as he climbed out of the broken drum and moved toward the audience and the aisle.

Stokowski stood immobile, arms folded, as Lundeen puffed past him.

Sunset and two other cops ran to the end of the stage, heading for the stairs.

Instruments were twanging, people were screaming, feet were running, but I could clearly hear Stokowski's voice as Lundeen turned and tried to bull past him, back to the stage. "You would take the money of musicians and war orphans!"

Lundeen ignored the Maestro, which proved to be a mistake. Stokowski threw a straight right at the company manager, who was thrusting out an arm to push him aside. The punch caught Lundeen's cheek. Lundeen turned on Stokowski, who hit the massive baritone in the nose with a right cross, following with an uppercut to the neck. Lundeen tried to level a punch at Stokowski, but the conductor beat him to it, throwing a solid left to the other's stomach. The punch split the seam of the hastily stitched uniform, and a rip up the side showed a hairy white leg.

"I've been in brawls with photographers, critics, the police, and musicians around the world. No baritone is a match for me," Stokowski said triumphantly, glancing back to be sure the audience had caught his performance. They had and were applauding.

I had my arms around Vera, watching. Sunset reached the platform and got a hand on Lundeen's pants' leg. Fighting off Stokowski with one hand, Lundeen kicked with his foot. The already torn pants came off in Sunset's hand.

. Letting out the bellow of a wild ape, Lundeen, in what was left of his Pinkerton uniform, leaped back into the orchestra pit and through the door under the stage through which most of the musicians had beat a retreat.

The cops went after him. Preston was the last one through

the door. He paused a beat to look up at me and shake his head.

It should have been the end, but it wasn't. The end is never really the end. The end is just where you decide to stop telling the story.

They didn't catch Lundeen, which, considering his physical condition, said little for the efficiency of the wartime San Francisco Police.

"Lot of places to hide," Preston said, coming back to Vera's dressing room, where I was taking off my makeup. "We've got the place surrounded, exits covered. We'll make a room-by-room search in the morning. You can pick up your wallet, gun, and car at the station."

"Thanks," I said.

"Come after ten," he suggested. "Sunset gets off at eight, and I don't think you want to run into him again."

"After ten," I agreed.

"Lot of things we can shut you up for," said Preston. "Moving Griffith's corpse, pulling the sword out of him, escaping from legal custody. Long list, but my chief doesn't want to see that Flores lawyer again. He's filed a defamation suit against the police department."

"I'll give Lundeen that," I said. "He got me a good lawyer when I needed one."

"Yeah," sighed Preston. "We'll be happy if you're out of town by noon tomorrow and you don't visit us again. It's a big country. I'll take San Francisco. You can have the rest."

"Sounds like a good deal."

"It is," he said. "We're clearing out the building. Twenty minutes. Out the front. No costumes. Single file."

He left us alone. Ten minutes later we met Shelly, Jeremy, Gunther, and Gwen in the front lobby. They were talking to Stokowski, who greeted Vera and me with a sad shake of his head.

"You would have been fine," he told her, taking her right hand in both of his. "I hope you were paid in advance."

"No," Vera said.

"I was. Always get paid in advance," Stokowski said.

"Maybe we can still . . ." Vera began.

"I'm afraid," Stokowski said with a sigh, "I must get back to New York. A crisis. Rumblings over my choice of music. Toscanini is doing battle for me, but I fear his heart is not in defending modern composers. Mr. Peters, I'm afraid a check will not be forthcoming for your services."

"Let's call my services a donation to art and culture," I said.

"I admire the gesture," he said with a bow. "I'll absorb the loss of Charles' uniform."

And he was gone.

"The man has good teeth," said Shelly.

"You should have told him, Shel," I said.

We agreed to meet in the late morning for breakfast at a place near Vera's hotel. Gunther, Jeremy, Shelly, and Gwen left single file through the main door.

Outside on the steps the Reverend Adam Souvaine was bullhorning to a crowd of about twenty, claiming victory for God, America, and the Church of the Enlightened Patriots. There were "Hallelujahs" and "Amens" and even a few cries of "Past the ammunition."

"See them emerge," Souvaine said, pointing up at us. His eyes, blazing with triumph, met mine. I looked at him steadily and smiled. He turned away and continued, "Like rats. The rotting edifice will crumble like the walls of Jericho, the temples of Babylon. God and his instruments, the Enlightened, will be ever alert whenever the Nazi snake or the yellow godless horde dare stick their heads above ground into the clean sunshine of America."

More shouts. The ancients danced and Vera bent her head to my ear.

"I'll call my agent tonight," she whispered, taking my hand.

"Maybe I'll have a few weeks or even more. I've never really seen Los Angeles."

"I'll show it to you," I offered.

"My makeup case," she exclaimed suddenly. "I left my makeup case in my dressing room."

We hurried back to get it, and that almost got us killed.

15

We were heading down the corridor outside the dressing rooms on our way back to the front of the building when the lights went out. We both stopped. I was carrying Vera's makeup bag. I shifted it to my left hand.

"Toby," Vera whispered. I found her hand.

"Power failure," I said.

"No," she said. "There's a light down there."

I wasn't sure where down there was, but I looked around and saw a vague glow. We headed for it.

"Straight down the hall," I said. "Nothing to trip over."

We moved slowly, the glow getting brighter, but not much. When we hit a door, I opened it and found the source of the glow, a dying bulb dangling from a wire snaking into the darkness above.

"Which way now?" I asked.

"That way, I think," Vera said, pointing that way.

As I took my first step in the direction she was pointing, two things happened. First, a man's voice began to sing, an echoing sound full of passion coming from the darkness in front of us. He was singing "Poor Butterfly." Second, the floor beneath us quivered. Plaster dust sprinkled down from the ceiling.

"What is it?" Vera asked, squeezing my hand.

"A tremor and a baritone," I said, wiping plaster from her hair.

"Deeper than baritone," Vera said. "I think I'm frightened."

"Hold your bag," I said. "I may need both hands free. And let's go."

We moved toward the singing and came to a stairway.

"Let's go back," Vera said.

"Let's just get out," I answered, and pulled her gently up the dark stairway.

We came to a landing. A small dirty window let in enough moonlight for us to see two doors and more steps going up.

The singing stopped and a deep voice came down the stairs.

"Are you familiar with William Blake, Peters?"

"Stop it," Vera shouted, putting one foot on the next step up.

"I can't," said the voice. "The game is not over. As Blake said, 'If you play a Game of Chance, know, before you begin, if you are benevolent you will never win.'"

A shot tore through the darkness and crackled the wallpaper near my head. I pushed through one of the doors and pulled Vera in with me. A large room. Another small window and even less moonlight. The vague beam hit a pair of doors across the room.

"'Great things are done when Men and Mountains meet,'" came the voice. "'This is not done by Jostling in the Street.'"

Footsteps were coming down the steps.

"You've made a wrong decision," came the voice on the opposite side of the door. "'The errors of a Wise Man make your Rule Rather than the Perfections of a Fool.'"

"Come on," I told Vera, and we worked our way across the room toward the pair of doors.

"Another choice," came the voice beyond the door behind us. "Two doors. Which will be the lady and which the tiger?"

I reached for one of the doors and threw it open. The moonlight fell on the dead white face of John Lundeen.

Vera screamed.

"Wrong choice," came the voice behind us.

Lundeen, still in his Pinkerton jacket, was hanging by the neck. He wore no pants, just a pair of white boxer shorts. The blue navy cap was perched on his head. I grabbed Vera and moved toward the second door.

The door behind us opened, and a flashlight beam shot over my shoulder as we went through the door next to the closet.

"One suicide and two disappearances," came the voice as I slammed the door behind us. "Or perhaps, two more murders and a remorseful suicide. I'll have to consider the many options."

A shot ripped through the wood and the man behind us launched into something in Italian. I didn't have time to ask Vera what it was, and she was in no condition to tell me.

We tripped down a narrow hallway and I pushed through the first door my hand touched, hoping it was a way out. It wasn't. We went through and I closed the door behind us. I could make out a ladder in the center of the room. I went for it, pulling Vera behind, and up we went as another slight tremor shook the building and set the chandelier waving.

And that's how I got into the situation I started this tale with.

Remember, I'd let go of the chandelier and dropped in the general direction of the Phantom, knowing I was going to miss him. As I jumped, a third tremor hit. Vera screamed above me. The Phantom fell backwards, and I landed on a section of the floor weak enough for one of my legs to go through up to the knee. Dust rose. My eyes were stinging, my leg in pain.

He was sitting dazed about six feet away from me. The flashlight was on the floor at his side, casting a beam in my direction. Also on the floor between us in the beam lay his fallen pistol.

I tried to pull my leg out of the floor, but I knew it was no go with the first pull. The leg was broken. I stretched for the gun. It was a good six inches out of reach.

"Toby," screamed Vera. "Are you all right?"

"Are you?" asked the Phantom, coming to his knees. He reached forward and pushed the gun toward me, just an inch or two, still out of my reach. "I would like to know that, too."

A ball of glass shattered near the flashlight. Then another. A third almost hit me. Vera was pulling glass teardrops from the chandelier and hurling them down.

The Phantom stopped the game and picked up the gun. He was still on his knees.

"Stop that," he shouted, "or I'll shoot him between the eyes."

Vera sobbed and stopped.

"Good," he whispered. "I keep my word. I'll shoot you in the heart. But first I'd like to know if you really knew who I was, or if I was simply being paranoid."

"Arthur Sullivan," I said, grinding my teeth against the pain, reaching around slowly out of the beam of light in hope of finding a board, a nail, something to use as a weapon. "You played Rance in the now-famous production of *La Fanciulla del West* in Cherokee seven years ago."

"Right," he said.

"You, Lundeen, and Lorna were involved in the death of the guy in the chorus."

"An accident," he said.

"Come on," I said, stalling while my fingers kept searching. "You're among enemies now." My eyes were adjusting to the near darkness.

"Well," he admitted, "not quite an accident."

"What are you doing down there?" cried Vera.

I could hear the chandelier swaying, tinkling, as she moved in the hope of seeing what was going on below her.

"Discussing history," the Phantom said.

"The three of you changed your names and went on to new identities," I said, holding back a groan of pain. "And then one of you, Lundeen probably, got the idea for duplicating the Texas scam here on a bigger scale."

"Good," said the Phantom. "But there were no photographs of me. When did you know?"

"When we went to Lundeen's office this morning," I said. "Outside the door."

"What did you hear?" he asked with interest.

"It's not what I heard," I said. "It's what I didn't hear. No raised voices. No quarrel. The second we opened the door, you and Lundeen were at it as if you'd been screaming at each other for an hour. Later, when we left the room, I could hear his normal voice on the phone behind the door. It gave me the idea that you and Lundeen had staged the argument."

"We did," admitted Adam Souvaine. "It really hadn't been a good plan, even from the beginning. I had a fair deal going with my flock when Johnny came to me. The money was fine, but his threat of exposure was even more convincing. I exhorted my flock against the opera while Johnny and Lorna worked from within. The irony is that we have ultimately succeeded, but we . . . or rather I, since I am the sole survivor of this bleak tontine . . . will collect nothing but my freedom—though my flock and I may receive a bit of credit for keeping the opera from opening. But we digress. Everyone who could have connected me to Texas or this fiasco is now dead, with the exception of you and the soprano."

"Toby," screamed Vera from above. "I can't hold on much longer."

"Patience," said Souvaine. "I'll have you down in a minute."

"The workman who died, Wyler?" I asked as Souvaine aimed the gun at my chest.

"Accident," said Souvaine.

"Lorna?" I asked.

"John's work, unplanned. She wanted out."

He pulled back the hammer.

"Griffith?"

"Mine," he said. "And let's call John a remorseful suicide."

"Let's."

"And we'll hide your body and that of our buxom young diva, and it will be the great mystery of the Opera," he said. "I'll claim that God took you. Better yet, I can write a suicide note from John saying he killed you before he took his own life. So many possibilities for a creative mind."

A small ball the size of a dog came hurtling out of the darkness from the direction of the door. Souvaine, still on his knees, was turning to the noise when Gunther landed on his neck, knocking him toward me. I reached up and grabbed Souvaine's arm. Gunther gave him a small-fisted punch in the face and I got the pistol.

Souvaine rose up on his knees and rolled Gunther across the room like a bowling ball. Vera screamed from above. On his feet now, he took a step toward Gunther. I aimed a few inches in front of his face and fired, not worrying too much about missing. He froze. Gwen came running through the door, saw what had happened, and rushed to Gunther, who was trying to sit up.

Souvaine threw back his cape and looked toward the door.

"Sit down," I said, aiming the gun at his stomach.

Souvaine sat. The events of the next ten minutes were worth recording on film. Gunther got up groggily and explained that he and Gwen had decided to wait for us to come out. When we didn't, they had come looking for us and had followed the sound of Souvaine's singing and the gunshots.

"You saved my life, Gunther," I said as he and Gwen grappled with the ladder and finally got it in position for Vera. When Vera got down, I gave the gun to Gunther, and the two women managed to pull me up through the floor. I couldn't walk. I could barely stay conscious. There was no feeling in my leg.

We all sat there exhausted for about five minutes before Vera and Gwen went for help.

I'll give Souvaine credit. He didn't offer a deal, make threats, or commit suicide by going for Gunther, who leveled the pistol at him with two steady hands.

"I could have been a first-rate character performer," said Souvaine. "If John hadn't been a fool in Texas . . . But life is a great 'if,' isn't it? And there is no grand finale. Beaten by a dwarf."

"A little person," I corrected, feeling Gunther bristle and imagining his finger tensing on the trigger.

Souvaine began to sing softly. He sang as Gwen and Vera returned, leading a trio of cops headed by Preston. He was still singing when I passed out as a couple of cops lifted me up.

In my delirium, Souvaine's voice became many voices and many songs. I was in a white room. Koko came in—wearing white—to work on my leg, assuring me with a grin and a wagging tongue that he'd have me as good as old in just a while.

And Souvaine's voice said, "Bullet scars, scar tissue still healing. Here. See?"

"It'll hurt for a year or two," said Koko, "and then it will go away."

And Souvaine's voice said, "The permanent discoloration is the result of an old hematoma, five years maybe, from multiple cracked ribs."

A line of people came to watch Koko operate on me with a sharp scalpel. People marched in single file, and I looked up at their distorted faces and heard their garbled voices.

And Souvaine's voice said, "No cartilage in the nose. Look. I don't know what these scratches on his chest, back, and leg are. They're recent, probably metal, nails, or barbed wire."

Stokowski pointed at my leg, taking the baton from Koko, and said I couldn't be in his orchestra if I had only one leg. "Nothing," he said, "should draw the audience's gaze from the conductor." He handed the baton back to Koko, saying he hadn't used one since 1921. Then he pulled the red leather-covered notebook from his pocket and made an entry about my leg.

And Souvaine's voice said, "Did you look at the X ray? The dislocation along the vertebrae? I'd like to look at this man's spleen."

He was followed by John Lundeen, dressed as a streetcar conductor, a transfer punch in his hand, wearing no pants. "Better the leg than the neck," he said, clicking his punch.

And Souvaine's voice said, "What the hell wars has this man been in?"

Lorna was next. She held a completely shaven Miguelito up to lick my face. Miguelito was covered with tattoos, names, phone numbers, ads for movies.

"Next," I said.

"Next what?" came Souvaine's voice.

"Next ghoul," I answered. "Next Phantom. Next ghost. Bring them on. I can take it. Any joke Koko's got for me, I can handle."

I opened my eyes and found myself looking into a craggy face.

"Your leg is broken," he said in Souvaine's voice. "Three places. I set it." His voice changed and sounded more like his face, craggy and deep. "My name's Doctor Ungurait. You've had a nightmare."

"No," I said. "It was the real thing."

16

Vera came to say good-bye the next morning. She was wearing a little black hat shaped like a "V." I was in a private room. I found out later she had paid for it. She leaned over to kiss my forehead and wake me from a dreamless nap.

"How are you?" she asked.

"Lovely."

She bit her lower lip.

"They're all dead," she said.

I wasn't sure whether she had read the morning *Chronicle* or was referring to Lorna, Griffith, and Lundeen. I nodded. I could tell from the fact that she was biting her lower lip that something other than death was on her mind.

"You're leaving," I said.

"I've got a possible . . . an audition for a new company in Seattle," she said. "My agent says we've got to get there by tomorrow."

"We?" I asked.

"Marty Passacaglia and me," she said, blushing. "His voice

173

is coming back, and he knows the major donator to the
company. Marty's not a bad person."

"Yes he is," I said.

"He and his wife aren't . . ." she began, but I stopped her.

"It's okay, Vera. I'm going back to Los Angeles tomorrow. If
you ever get there, look me up in the phone book under
Private Investigators or Dentists."

"I will," she said with a tear in the very corner of her left eye.

I reached for a Kleenex. The move hurt my leg. She dabbed
at her eyes daintily. I was sure I'd seen her rehearse this scene
the day before.

"You're going to be a star," I said. If she could do Cio-
cio-san, I could do Norman Maine in *A Star is Born.*

"Wherever I go," she said, "the tragedy of the past days will
haunt my career."

"Let's hope so," I said. "A legend like this must be great for
an opera singer."

The smile came. "Good-bye, Toby."

I dabbed the corner of my eye with a Kleenex and she
laughed, a very musical laugh, and was gone.

About ten minutes later Lawyer Flores showed up, dressed
in his finest, carrying his briefcase. He surveyed my crushed
and scarred body and shook his head a few times.

"All charges against you have been dropped," he said. "If
you like, I can institute a charge of false arrest, which I will take
on a contingency basis for 50 percent of all restitution. I advise
you, however, not to institute such charges, since they will
bring up the fact of your escape from custody, which was
illegal whether or not you were guilty. Still, I think we could get
the police to settle out of court."

"Forget it," I said.

"Good," said Flores, opening his briefcase. "That will make
it easier to pursue my case. I'd like you to read the statement
I have prepared for your signature, and sign it."

I read. It was a statement saying I had heard Inspector

Sunset insult Flores and his cultural background and ethnicity. I signed.

"You think you can win this?" I asked him when he took back the signed statement and pen.

"No," he said, "but I can make an issue of it. I can make an issue each time, and if enough of us make an issue, it will stop. In return for your cooperation in this matter, I will not bill you for my services."

"Thanks," I said.

We shook hands and he left.

I listened to the radio the rest of the day. I slept through *Mystery Man*, answered a few questions on *Quick as a Flash*, had a few chuckles with Henry Aldrich and Homer, who tried to find a way for Henry to earn enough money to take a new girl at school to the big dance. I liked the way Ezra Stone's voice cracked. It soothed me to sleep.

In the morning, Gunther, Shelly, and Jeremy arrived. I didn't like it, but the only one of the trio who could drive my Crosley was Shelly. Jeremy couldn't fit into the driver's seat and it wasn't propped up for Gunther, who informed me that Gwen would, indeed, be attempting to transfer from San Francisco University to the University of Southern California at the end of the semester to complete her graduate work.

"This is not a good town for a creative dentist," Shelly complained as Jeremy picked me up out of the bed. Shelly trotted at our side. Gunther moved ahead opening doors. We hit the sidewalk in front of the hospital; my Crosley and Gunther's Daimler were parked at the curb. Shelly went on, "The people who most need serious oral care keep murdering each other, leaving town, or going to jail. In Los Angeles, they stay put. I think my plan for branching out into dog dental hygiene has promise here, though."

"Right, Shel," I said. "Drive carefully."

I'm not sure if Shelly answered. He climbed into my Crosley, ground the gears, and pulled away. Jeremy put me in the back

seat of the Daimler, put my suitcase on the floor, and joine
Gunther in front.

We drove through town and over the Oakland Bay Bridge
I sat with my legs on the seat and my back to the window.
drifted in and out of sleep and ate a sandwich with a Peps
somewhere along the way. I tried to read Mrs. Plaut's manu
script for a while, but darkness came. I popped a pill Do
Ungurait had given me and sweated off to sleep.

Sometime during the night we went through Santa Barbara
and the next morning we hit Los Angeles and drove t
Heliotrope. Jeremy lifted me from the back seat and carrie
me down the walk and up the steps to the porch, where Mrs
Plaut stood, hands in apron pockets, blinking at us.

"Mr. Peelers," she said. "You court disaster."

"It would so appear, Mrs. Plaut," I said as Gunther hurrie
ahead and opened the screen door.

"Your cat did not eat my bird," she said.

"I'm pleased," I said.

"But my bird died of the apoplexy," she continued, followin
us.

"I'm sorry," I said as Gunther went up the stairs and Jerem
followed with me in his arms.

"I believe the apoplexy was caused by a fear of your cat
she called.

"Are you sure it was apoplexy?" I called back.

"It was a yellow canary," she said with exasperation at m
lack of basic feathered epidemiology.

"Ah," I said, looking down at her from the top of the stai
where Jeremy had paused so that Mrs. Plaut and I cou
continue our brilliant repartee.

"I do not blame the cat," she said. "He attempted to be
gentleman. It was the sight of the innocent creature that dor
birdie in. The memory of the species is built in like
carburetor. Did you shoot anyone this outing?"

"No," I said.

"Did you read my chapter?" she asked as Gunther came o

of my room to announce softly that he had unpacked my bag.

"I have a few pages to go," I admitted, with a whisper to Jeremy to get me into my room.

"Do you not believe that Cousin Pyle's encounter with Sitting Bull in the Baptist church in Cherokee was good stuff?" she asked.

I touched Jeremy's shoulder to stop him. Since I seemed to be no burden to him I felt only a slight touch of guilt.

"Cherokee, Texas?" I asked.

"Family tree's from there," she said. "Cousin Pyle's branch. Cousin Pyle was not my cousin but the cousin of my mother. I visited them often with the Mister."

"Ever hear of an opera there?" I asked.

Gunther had gone back into my room.

"No opera in Cherokee," she said emphatically. "Tried to do one a few years back. Cousin Pyle was sheriff. The opera people absconded with the receipts. Since that night, both Cherokee and the Plauts have refused to enter an opera house, though I do sometimes listen to Milton Cross on Saturdays."

"I'm tired, Mrs. Plaut," I said, looking at Jeremy. "And in awe of the way the gods tie our lives together in knots. Until two days ago, I had never heard of Cherokee, Texas. Now it's haunting me."

"Then sleep," she said.

"Hearing aid's working fine," I added.

Mrs. Plaut smiled, and Jeremy carried me into my room and put me on the mattress, which Gunther had apparently wrestled to the floor.

"What are the odds of running into someone from Cherokee, Texas?" I said.

"It is not a coincidence," Jeremy said, gently helping Gunther take off my clothes. "It is, like the process of birth, part of the mystery of being, of life. We are seldom receptive to seeing the silken links that bind us together."

I could hear the phone ring in the hall and Mrs. Plaut's footsteps start up the stairs.

"God's got one heck of a sense of humor," I said, trying to prop myself up.

"I too have noticed that," said Jeremy.

"I will be in my room, Toby," Gunther said. There were little dark circles under his eyes and his tie was slightly loose. He was tired from driving all night but also buoyed by the thought of Gwen of San Francisco coming to Los Angeles. "Please knock on the floor with your shoe should you need anything. I will return with a late lunch."

"Thanks, Gunther," I said.

Gunther bowed and exited. Mrs. Plaut was standing in the doorway holding Dash in her arms. She let the cat leap to the floor. He ran to me and began to use my cast as a scratching post.

"I had almost forgotten," Mrs. Plaut said. "A woman in a funny hat came to the door two days ago and left you this."

She handed me a pink envelope with an eye painted on it. Dash furiously continued to scratch while Mrs. Plaut watched. My leg began to itch under the cast where Dash was scratching.

"Cats," she said.

"Cats," I agreed and opened the envelope. The paper inside was red with green lettering which said:

> I cannot understand why man should be capable of so little fantasy. I do not understand why, when I ask for a grilled lobster in a restaurant, I am never served a cooked telephone; I do not understand why champagne is always chilled, and why on the other hand telephones, which are habitually so frightfully warm and disagreeably sticky to the touch, are not also put in silver buckets with crushed ice around them. Please try to locate a telephone which does not offend you and call me at the number below. I am in need of your services.

There was a phone number and a signature.
"Who's it from?" asked Mrs. Plaut.
"Salvador Dalí," I said.
"The king of Tibet!" she said with awe.
I closed my eyes and went to sleep.

THE END

MORE MYSTERIOUS PLEASURES

Order #	Titles	Price
	HAROLD ADAMS	*The Carl Wilcox series*
501	MURDER	$3.95
601	PAINT THE TOWN RED	$3.95
602	THE MISSING MOON	$3.95
420	THE NAKED LIAR	$3.95
502	THE FOURTH WIDOW	$3.50
603	THE BARBED WIRE NOOSE	$3.95
901	THE MAN WHO MISSED THE PARTY	$4.95
	THOMAS ADCOCK	
902	SEA OF GREEN	$4.95
	TED ALLBEURY	
604	THE SEEDS OF TREASON	$3.95
802	THE JUDAS FACTOR	$4.50
903	THE LANTERN NETWORK	$4.95
904	ALL OUR TOMORROWS	$4.95
	ERIC AMBLER	
701	HERE LIES: AN AUTOBIOGRAPHY	$8.95
	KINGSLEY AMIS	
905	THE CRIME OF THE CENTURY	$4.95
	ROBERT BARNARD	
702	A TALENT TO DECEIVE: AN APPRECIATION OF AGATHA CHRISTIE	$8.95

Order #	Titles	Price

JIM THOMPSON

538	THE KILL-OFF	$3.95
641	THE NOTHING MAN	$3.95
642	BAD BOY	$3.95
643	ROUGHNECK	$3.95
831	THE GOLDEN GIZMO	$3.95
832	THE RIP-OFF	$3.95
833	FIREWORKS: THE LOST WRITINGS	$4.50

COLIN WATSON

722	SNOBBERY WITH VIOLENCE: CRIME STORIES AND THEIR AUDIENCES	$8.95

DONALD E. WESTLAKE

541	THE BUSY BODY	$3.95
542	THE SPY IN THE OINTMENT	$4.95
543	GOD SAVE THE MARK	$3.95
834	DANCING AZTECS	$4.95
835	TWO MUCH!	$4.95
836	*HELP* I AM BEING HELD PRISONER	$4.50
837	TRUST ME ON THIS	$4.50
941	SACRED MONSTER	$4.95
942	TOMORROW'S CRIMES	$4.95

The Dortmunder series

539	THE HOT ROCK	$3.95
540	BANK SHOT	$4.95
838	JIMMY THE KID	$3.95
839	NOBODY'S PERFECT	$3.95

TERI WHITE

544	TIGHTROPE	$3.95
840	FAULT LINES	$4.50

PHYLLIS A. WHITNEY

841	THE RED CARNELIAN	$4.50

COLLIN WILCOX *The Lt. Frank Hastings series*

545	NIGHT GAMES	$3.95
842	THE PARIAH	$4.95

Order #	Titles	Price

DAVID WILLIAMS   *The Mark Treasure series*

| 112 | UNHOLY WRIT | $3.95 |
| 113 | TREASURE BY DEGREES | $3.95 |

GAHAN WILSON

| 843 | EVERYBODY'S FAVORITE DUCK | $4.95 |

CORNELL WOOLRICH/LAWRENCE BLOCK

| 646 | INTO THE NIGHT | $3.95 |

- -

AVAILABLE AT YOUR BOOKSTORE OR DIRECT FROM THE PUBLISHER

Mysterious Press Mail Order
129 West 56th Street
New York, NY 10019

Please send me the MYSTERIOUS PRESS paperback titles below:

Order #	Title	Price

Please add another page for additional titles.

Shipping [ ]

CREDIT CARD # _____

Circle One: AM EX. VISA. MC   Exp. Date _____

TOTAL [ ]

I am enclosing $_____ (please add $3.00 postage and handling for the first book, and 50¢ for each additional book.) Send check, money order or credit card only—no cash or COD please. Allow 4 weeks for delivery.

NAME _____

ADDRESS _____

CITY _____ STATE _____ ZIP CODE _____

New York State residents please add appropriate sales tax.